Praise for Kim Slater:

'A remarkable first novel' *Guardian* on *Smart*

'It made me see the world in a different way' Ellen, age 12, for lovereading4kids.co.uk on *Smart*

'Kim Slater has struck gold again . . . a moving and uplifting novel' *School Librarian* on *A Seven-Letter Word*

'Pace, wit, pathos and humour in a book that looks and feels engaging' *Carousel* on *A Seven-Letter Word*

'Powerful and thought-provoking . . . Kim Slater's message on diversity is loud and clear' ReadingZone on *928 Miles from Home*

'[A] warm, truthful and insightful depiction of working-class life' lovereading4kids.co.uk on *928 Miles from Home*

'A fast-paced mystery with plenty of twists and turns but it's also a heartfelt and powerful piece of social commentary' *The Bookbag* on *The Boy Who Lied*

Books by Kim Slater

Smart

A Seven-Letter Word

928 Miles from Home

The Boy Who Lied

A SEVEN LETTER WORD

KIM SLATER

MACMILLAN CHILDREN'S BOOKS

First published 2016 by Macmillan Children's Books

This edition published 2019 by Macmillan Children's Books
an imprint of Pan Macmillan
20 New Wharf Road, London N1 9RR
Associated companies throughout the world
www.panmacmillan.com

ISBN 978-1-5290-0920-0

1 3 5 7 9 8 6 4 2

A CIP catalogue record for this book is available from the British Library.

Printed and bound by CPI Group (UK) Ltd, Croydon CR0 4YY

Author's Note

All Scrabble references and scores have been researched and calculated to
the best of my knowledge and ability, but I am not a professional player,
so please note that any potential errors, however unintentional,
will remain as they are for consistency from edition to edition.
Kim Slater

This book is dedicated in loving memory of my nana, Gladys Sherwin, who is forever in my heart

Monday, 11 May
Dear Mum,

It's me, Finlay.

I've had this brilliant idea to empty out all the words in my head on to paper. That way, they might stop driving me bonkers, buzzing around with no way of getting out.

I'm writing in the journal I found in the box of your things that I managed to save from Dad's manic FUMIGATION [16] session when you left. I hope you don't mind; you never wrote anything in it.

Seeing as I'm using your journal, I thought it made sense that I write directly to *you*.

For starters, I know you'll appreciate the Scrabble scores I'm giving for the best words. I practise every day just like you taught me, and my vocabulary is improving all the time. I've come on a lot since we used to play together.

I wish I could show you, Mum. I think you'd be proud.

Course, I didn't have to write to you, I know that. I could've wrote to . . . well anybody, really, but I don't know that many people since we moved house.

It's much easier to get your feelings out when you know someone well. Or *used* to know someone well. And daft as it sounds, it helps me feel closer to you.

I still think about us every single day, our family.

I know none of us were perfect. Probably I could've

1

been better behaved, and when you used to ask if I'd tidied my bedroom or done my homework, I wish now I'd listened.

But I didn't know what was going to happen, did I? I didn't try harder because I thought things were safe. I thought things would always be the same.

I break up from school next Friday, for spring half-term holiday. I don't know how I'm going to fill every day stuck at home for a whole week but it's going to help, now I can write to you.

Only, if I wrote how I speak, I'd need a full sheet of this journal for every sentence and you'd soon get fed up with that.

See, I'm a different lad to the one you left behind.

I can see OK, can hear perfectly fine and I can write really well. But the thing is, I can't speak. It's not just the odd word any more.

I'm a st-st-stutterer.

STUTTER [7] – that's one seven-letter word I wish didn't exist, fifty points extra or not.

Hilarious, isn't it?

It's like the word is there in my mouth, fully formed, and then, just as it's ready to leave my lips . . . POP! It ricochets and bounces around my gob.

Except it's not funny at all, because there's not a damn thing I can do about it.

Worst of all, people think I'm totally and utterly

stupid. I mean, speaking is the most natural thing in the world to do. And that's the hardest thing to take, I suppose, because I want to be bright and clever and ARTICULATE [12]. Like you.

I'm not telling you this to make you feel bad, Mum, honest.

You see, I've made my mind up to write anything I want to down here. My journal letters to you will be UNCENSORED [13].

If I'm going to write the truth, it's the only way.

And anyway, you'll never get to read any of this stuff because like Dad says, when you left, you were gone forever from our lives.

He says you might as well be dead.

Love,

Finlay x

SCRABBLE IS A POPULAR WORD GAME THAT IS PLAYED WITH ONE HUNDRED TILES.

Tuesday

I hear Dad clattering about downstairs, which means breakfast is nearly ready.

I wrap Mum's journal up in my pyjama top and slide it into my T-shirt drawer.

I check Neville's water bottle and then I go downstairs before Dad shouts at me, save him having one of his coughing fits. He usually leaves the house before I get up, but today he's fitting a kitchen in a house just two streets away, so he's leaving a bit later.

Dad is puffing away and stirring something on the cooker. He turns round and puts two plates down on the table, angling his head so fag ash doesn't drop from his mouth.

Breakfast is the same as last night's tea: egg and beans but without the chips.

He puts another plate down with three pieces of buttered white toast on it. Mum used to slice them

4

diagonally into triangles. Silly, I know, but toast always seem to taste nicer, cut like that.

I make two mugs of tea and we both sit down.

Dad has forgotten the ketchup and gets up again. I really fancy some brown sauce but he has his back to me at the cupboard.

'D-Da-Da—'

It's just a flipping three-letter word: D-A-D.

It's even rubbish points on the Scrabble board because it's so simple.

DAD. *Just say it.*

'Da-Da-Dad.'

He turns around with the bottle of ketchup in his hand.

I look at him. He looks back at me.

'I w-want s-some –'

I always worry that Dad will get annoyed but he hardly ever does.

I stop and swallow hard. I still haven't finished the sentence.

My lower back is wet. My throat hurts.

'Bloody hell, Finlay.' Dad strides over. 'Are we going to get this food down us while it's still hot, or what?'

I nod.

'Here, ketchup.' He plonks it down on the table. 'Is that what you're after?'

I don't say anything.

5

We start to eat. Dad pushes his plate to the right-hand side a touch, so he can spread his paper out better.

The wall clock has a loud tick and I can hear the grill pan creaking and snapping as it cools.

Dad laughs out loud at something he's just read and I get a good view of the chewed-up egg and chips that's still sitting on top of his tongue.

'What?' He stops chewing and looks at me.

I want to tell Dad about the new two-letter Scrabble words I learned last night and about my decision to write to Mum. I want him to tell me it's OK that I couldn't get the words out earlier.

I look down at my plate and I don't say anything.

'Pass that egg over here if you don't want it then, lad,' he says, with his mouth still full.

OF THE ONE HUNDRED LETTERED TILES IN PLAY, TWO ARE BLANK.

The school bus is late and within a few minutes, a big queue has formed behind me.

There's a light drizzle and a bit of a chill in the early morning air but the weather is getting warmer.

My rucksack feels heavy and uncomfortable on my back. There are four thick library books in there, all overdue. I'm just debating whether to start walking to the next bus stop when I hear his voice behind me.

'F-F-Finlay!'

There's a pounding of feet as Oliver Haywood and his mob approach the bus stop.

I don't realize I've stopped breathing until I start to feel a bit dizzy. I take in a gulp of air but I don't turn around. They've never caught the bus from this stop before, it's like they've come here just to start on me.

Oliver calls out again, louder this time.

'F-flipping heck, it's F-Finlay.'

They ignore the queue and walk straight to the front

to gather round me. They all wear their ties done loose with sloppy knots and Oliver has a swirly design shaved into one side of his hair. He's got this concerned look on his face.

'You OK, F-Finlay? It m-must be fl-flaming f-freezing, stood here.'

Everybody laughs. Even the other kids who hardly know me.

'This is really serious,' Oliver says, in a worried voice. 'It looks like F-Finlay M-McIntosh has turned deaf, as well as dumb. Do you reckon he needs a bit of a shock to bring him out of it?'

People jeer and laugh, making one big, mixed-up sound. Bright eyes and neat teeth flash all around me.

There's a very small tuft of grass at the bottom of the bus-stop pole that has somehow managed to survive the pounding of thousands of boots and shoes. I imagine myself shrinking down next to it so I'm almost invisible.

For a second or two, the noise around me fades far away.

I don't expect the blow that sends me careering head first into the steel pole. A sharp pain bounces around the inside of my skull. I can feel Oliver pulling at my rucksack and all I can think is that my Scrabble tile bag is in there, the one Mum made before she left.

Someone pulls my left arm back – the noise level ramps up – and I feel the rucksack completely slip off one side. I don't even think about it, I just fling my other arm up quick before the rucksack can completely slip off and smash my elbow backwards to push everyone away. My bag smacks hard into someone behind me. Before I even realize what I've done, Oliver's on the ground, groaning and clutching his shoulder.

I forgot about the library books. I just clobbered Oliver with the full swinging weight of them.

The laughter stops. I glance around and lots of eyes look back at me; some are glaring, some curious, and some even have a hint of admiration.

There's a heavy diesel rumble and a whoosh of air brakes. I've never been so glad to see the school bus. The doors hiss and open, and I jump on, flashing my bus pass at the driver and sitting down heavily, as far away from the pavement windows as I can.

As the bus pulls away I glance back to see Oliver staggering to his feet and glaring in at me, his face tight and pinched as he rubs his shoulder and shrugs off his mates who are trying to help him.

Just before I look away, he slides one finger across his throat in a cutting motion.

THE SCRABBLE BOARD IS MADE UP OF SMALLER, INDIVIDUAL BOXES THAT MAKE UP ONE LARGE, SQUARE GRID.

Soon as I get home from school, I'm just waiting until I can clear away the tea and escape upstairs.

'That's a nasty bruise on your forehead,' Dad says, putting down his mug and peering at me. 'How did you come by that?'

I press the swelling a bit too hard and flinch.

'I tr-tripped,' I say. 'A-at the b-b-b—'

'Bus stop?'

I nod.

'Like the arm of your blazer got torn at the bus stop?' Dad frowns.

I look away.

I've spent all day waiting to be called to the Head of Year's office for hurting Oliver. When he reports me, I'll probably get excluded from school.

Dad clears his throat. 'I didn't fall off a Christmas tree, you know, lad. If somebody's giving you bother, I want to know about it.'

'I-I'm f-fine,' I say. I stack our greasy plates in the sink and edge towards the hallway. Dad means well but he doesn't understand how things work at school.

Upstairs in my bedroom, I turn on my computer.

While it's booting up I watch the 5.45 train zip past on its way to Lincoln. Our house is right next to the railway tracks, so even though we've got double glazing, you can still really hear it.

I can see the bobbing heads of all the commuters heading home at the end of their long day. I bet they're thinking about what they're going to have for tea or watch on TV later, they might be planning how they'll spend their wages at the end of the month. I'd much rather be at work than at school.

When me and Dad first moved to Colwick, I used to sit right here in my bedroom for hours, logging the times of the trains. I even designed a proper sheet, so it looked neat and professional.

I didn't do anything with the pages and pages of numbers, but it felt really important at the time. If I missed logging a train, I felt all panicky. Like something bad was going to happen.

One night Dad asked me what I was doing, so I showed him the lists. After that he bought me a computer – and that's when I found out there was a whole online community out there, playing Scrabble.

Me and Mum used to play Scrabble all the time. If Dad was watching football in the living room, me and Mum would set the board up on the kitchen table.

Now I play online with different people from all over the world. This week, there's been Todd from Kansas, Markus from Germany, Jasminder from India, and Sarah from London. Secretly, I think that Markus might be cheating. Some of the words he comes up with, even I haven't heard of.

There's no chit-chat or messing about, we just get on with playing the game. The other players don't know anything about me at all. They haven't got a clue that I can't even say my own name or string a sentence together.

I'd like to be that boy in real life.

You know where you stand, playing Scrabble online; there are never any surprises.

Except tonight.

Tonight when I sit in front of the screen, there's a player waiting for me. Which wouldn't be that unusual, apart from the fact it's not one of my regular group. It is someone completely new.

A message window pops up.

Hi . . . I'm Alex. Want to play?

Why not? Fresh competition is always good.

OK, I reply. **I'm Finlay.**

We begin play and Alex is quite good. But I have a decent rack of tiles.

A scratching noise distracts me but it's only Neville, pootling out of his little house. Hamsters are what you call *crepuscular* animals, which means that Neville is usually out and about during the twilight hours. Depending on his mood, he is awake between about eight in the evening until three or four in the morning, and that's when I get to chat with him about my day.

'Evening, Neville,' I call.

He looks over and twitches his nose. He's my best friend and I don't care if that sounds crazy. Neville doesn't give a toss how I speak and I don't care that he doesn't speak at all. We understand each other perfectly.

Soon, Alex's score is lagging. We're both coming up with standard words and there's nothing unusual about the game at all.

Until the message box pops up again, twelve minutes in.

I'm knackered from football training, but I'm not making excuses, you're really good. How long have you been playing, Finlay?

Chit-chat is frowned upon during both face-to-face and online play. No talking, which suits me just fine.

I stare at the message box and the words in it. It has blocked off part of the board.

It's my turn. I was planning to play M-O-C-K-E-D,

using the D of one of Alex's words and placing the K, worth five points, on a double-letter square. But I've already forgotten the exact letter layout and the total points I'll score.

Before it affects my game any more, I click on the tiny cross up at the top right and close the message box down. I play my letters and wait for Alex to play his word.

Within seconds, the box pops up again.

How long have you been playing for, Finlay?

I tap in my reply.

Since I was six.

Maybe he'll stop chattering now.

Another couple of turns each and then I play my next word that gets me forty-two points and brings the score to 278–199, my favour.

That's when the box appears again.

You're REALLY good! Soz for delay, went to make a cuppa but could only find this weird lapsang souchong stuff ☺ !

My stomach lurches. I'd forgotten about that tea, the strong smell of it. Mum used to drink it all the time. I thought it smelt of old kippers.

Great to find an online pal, Alex types.

I'd hardly call us mates, we've only been playing for nineteen minutes.

Got no mates at sch, he says. **Glad I've met you!**

I think about telling Alex I know how that feels but

14

I'll sound like a loser. I like how he seems to be looking up to me.

That must be tough, I reply.

Another turn each and that should complete the game.

Where do you live? he asks. **Just rough area.**

Alarm bells start jangling in my head.

Be great if we could be mates in real life, he continues.

Might as well be straight about it, whether it offends him or not.

Sorry, don't exchange personal details, I type.

He's getting Scrabble confused with a chat forum.

No probs. I'm not a 40-year-old psycho . . . honest!

I grin at that. Maybe I'm being too paranoid. Alex seems all right, but he'll never improve his game if he keeps chattering on.

The Scrabble clock clicks to 20:00 minutes. Game over.

My fingers hover over the keyboard to say goodbye but the message box has disappeared. He's already logged off.

I sit on the floor in front of Neville's cage, open the door and scoop his warm body into my hand.

'Do you think I've found a new friend, Neville?' I ask him.

I settle him on my stretched-out legs and he sits back

on his hind paws and looks up at me. 'Don't look at me like that.' I grin. 'We're n-not all anti-social like you. Having friends is a good thing when you're a human.'

Syrian hamsters, like Neville, are solitary animals. They'll fight if they have to share their cage, sometimes to the death. But Russian hamsters become very close with their mates and get depressed if they're separated. Which is quite nice, I think, in a funny sort of way.

I would be like a Russian hamster if I were a rodent. There's no fun in being lonely all of your life.

Tuesday, 12 May
Dear Mum,

It's very late, but before I go to sleep, I want to tell you what happened today.

Oliver had a go at me again, but this time I got him good. I whacked him with my rucksack, and I think I might have disjointed his shoulder or something because in the afternoon, I spotted him across the playground with his arm in a sling. I know you won't approve, Mum, but you don't know what he's like. He totally deserved it, so I've decided not to waste any more time worrying about it. Which is harder to do than it sounds.

I keep wondering if he's going to report me to Mr Homer, though. I won't deny it if he does, but if I tell Mr Homer the truth about how Oliver makes my life a misery every day, Dad will get involved and then everything will get even worse. I'll just say I hit Oliver and that will be that. Anyway, like I say, I'm not worrying about it. Honest.

Something good happened today, too. I met this new player online. His name is Alex. I'm not sure why, but for some reason, I think that maybe, just maybe, we might become proper friends in real life. He sounds like he might be going through the same stuff I am at school and he seemed really interested in me.

If you were here, you'd probably say I had an

over-active imagination. You'd be sitting at the kitchen table studying your sales figures. And you'd be drinking that horrible tea you like – *lapsang souchong*.

Weirdly, that's one of the strange things Alex mentioned.

It got me thinking about how I used to come downstairs to run my homework by you or tell you something about my day.

You always listened.

Dad isn't a very good listener and he won't listen to any talk at all about you. He even gets annoyed if other people mention you.

Like the time Dr Khan referred me to a speech therapist just after you'd left us. She didn't give me any exercises to help with my stutter; she just asked a lot of questions, and most of them didn't have anything to do with speaking at all.

Afterwards, when Dad went in, I had to wait outside her office – but he didn't shut the door properly. I heard her telling him that you leaving so suddenly could be the reason my stutter had got so much worse, so quickly.

Dad stormed out and yanked me up from the chair. He gripped my hand so tight I thought my bones would be permanently BUCKLED [16]. I had to run beside him just to keep my fingers attached.

He said he wasn't angry. But he looked it.

Then he asked if I fancied a burger and a milkshake

and to sit by the canal for a while.

I said no because his voice sounded stretched and a bit high and I could see that the twitch in his jaw had started, like it used to when you two had an argument.

When we got home, I wished I'd said yes because there was only egg and beans for tea. Anyway, after all that, he just put the footy on TV and seemed completely normal again.

These days, Dad's so busy with work, he's got no time for anything at all. He comes home to make our tea, wolfs down his food and then goes back out again until late. Sometimes, he falls asleep in his chair all night without taking his coat and boots off. He says he's got to take the work while it's there, now it's just me and him, looking after each other.

Things are fine at home, so don't go worrying about us.

Since I learned how to iron in our Home Skills lessons, nobody laughs at my school shirts because I don't wear them all creased up any more.

Love,

Finlay x

THE PLAYING GRID IS SIZED EXACTLY FIFTEEN SQUARES HIGH AND FIFTEEN CELLS WIDE.

Wednesday

I don't mind that it's raining heavily. I'm just glad I've managed to get through the day without running into Oliver and his cronies.

Since Dad spotted the bruise on my forehead yesterday, he's decided he's going to pick me up in the evenings, like I'm still at primary school.

I waited in the toilets until I knew all the school buses had left before I came outside to wait for my lift.

Dad knows other kids tease me about my stammer. He gets really angry about it and sometimes he even tells me I should just thump whoever is giving me bother.

Once, he even showed me how to make a proper fist like a boxer, so I don't break my thumb when I punch someone. Dad can't seem to understand I'm not like he was when he was a lad.

He'd probably be pleased if he knew I'd clobbered Oliver yesterday, but then I'd have to explain what Oliver was doing at the time.

I watch up the road for Dad's white van to appear, with *'Paul McIntosh, Your Local Plumber* – no job to big or to small!' emblazoned on the side. He'd painted the sign himself, to save money. When Mum spotted the spelling mistakes, Dad tried to paint in the two missing O's, but it looked all squashed up and messy. He said it didn't even matter because most people around here wouldn't know it was the wrong spelling in the first place.

But Mum refused to go out in Dad's van after that, even to Aldi to do the food shopping.

A text pings through. I pull my phone from my blazer pocket, shielding it from the rain with my other hand.

Will be about 30 mins late, delayed on a job. Sorry, Dad.

Great. There's no point waiting out here and getting soaked through – so I dash back inside and head for the library on the first floor.

It feels really weird in school when everyone has gone home but I kind of like it. My footsteps echo on the metal-trimmed stairs and I don't have to keep looking over my shoulder to check if Oliver is behind me.

When I get to the first floor, a mildewy stink mixes with the earthy rain that's trickling in through the old metal-framed windows. I stop for a moment and dip my finger into a pool of rainwater that has settled on the inside windowsill like a splash of silver paint.

You wouldn't think it to look at it, but rainwater is

mildly acidic and over a period of time, it can disintegrate even the toughest rock. 'Disintegration' is a long word, but it would only be worth sixteen points on the Scrabble board.

Most people think that

Supercalifragilisticexpialidocious

is the longest word in English. It comes from the *Mary Poppins* musical, contains thirty-four letters and is worth fifty-six points. But I know a longer word:

Pneumonoultramicroscopicsilicovolcanokoniosis.

Pneumonoultramicroscopicsilicovolcanokoniosis is a technical term for lung disease caused by breathing in silica dust. It's very nasty. It has forty-five letters in it and is worth seventy points. But as you only ever have seven letters to play with in Scrabble, you could never play any of these words in real life. Knowing they even exist at all is a bit frustrating.

I push open the library doors and step into the warmth. Hushed voices are coming over from the far corner behind the bookcases where Mrs Adams, the school librarian, stands. She's got eyes like a hawk that are really good for spotting people who are messing about or defacing books.

'Nice to see you, Finlay.' She says it loud and slow, as if I were deaf. Or stupid. Or both.

'I hope there are no more overdue library books in that rucksack?'

I shake my head and wonder if Oliver has grassed me up yet.

'Have you come for the club?'

I shake my head.

'Well, it's your lucky afternoon.' She beams, beckoning me to follow her.

I'd like to sit in a quiet corner, spill out my Scrabble tiles and practise anagrams like I always do when I get any free time in the library, but instead, I follow Mrs Adams.

She leads me behind the bookcases, where a group of students are sitting quietly around three or four tables. Two sixth-formers shuffle around the groups, watching.

'We're one player short,' Mrs Adams points to a spotty Year 10 boy sitting alone, who I've seen around school.

It's then I realize this is the Scrabble after-school club.

I take a step back.

'Come on,' she chides me. 'Don't be nervous. Liam will teach you how to play, won't you, Liam?'

Liam shrugs.

I want to tell her that my dad will be here very soon and that, anyway, I only play online, but the words are bunching up in my throat, so I seal my lips before I make a complete fool of myself.

'I know you'd like to have a go at Scrabble, I've seen

you playing with your tiles in here before,' Mrs Adams says.

Everyone is listening. I feel a trickle of sweat slide down the hollow at the bottom of my back. I can't just stand here in silence.

'I d-d—'

'You do? That's good. Sit down there and Liam will explain the game. OK, Liam?'

'But miss, I—'

'Just do it, Liam.'

'I'll give him a game, miss,' a familiar voice calls from behind me. 'In the interests of good sportsmanship and all that.'

I turn around to see Oliver Haywood walking across the library towards us.

My face and neck begin to prickle.

'That's very admirable, Oliver,' Mrs Adams says, scowling at Liam. 'You're a lucky boy, Finlay. Oliver began studying the game as part of his Duke of Edinburgh Award and now he's our star player. If he carries on improving, he's in with a chance of representing us at the championships in a few weeks' time.'

It feels like I'm watching myself from a distance, like it's all happening in slow motion. Oliver is a sports fanatic; I never had him down as a geeky board-game player.

I feel cornered, like a rat in a cage but there's nothing I can do.

Liam skulks off and Oliver sits down, never taking his eyes off me.

'I'll do my best to teach him, miss,' he says slowly, glancing down at his sling. 'Even though my shoulder is *really hurting*.'

EACH LETTER TILE EARNS A
DIFFERENT SCORE WHEN PLAYED.

As soon as Mrs Adams walks away, Oliver leans forward and grabs my wrist hard with his good hand.

'I'll paste you into the ground, you little freak,' he hisses, digging his fingers into the soft tissue of my forearm. 'Not just at Scrabble, either. I'll get you back when you least expect it, for knackering up my shoulder.'

He looks around, checks nobody is listening. 'I suppose you're wondering why Homer's not called you into his office?'

I shrug my shoulders. I won't give him the satisfaction of seeing he's got me worried.

'It's because I haven't grassed you up, that's why.'

I wait. I know there's more coming.

'I'll give out my own punishment when I'm ready.' He grins and jabs his fingers in harder.

I snatch my arm free and pick up the tile bag, giving it a shake.

'Choose some g-good letters, F-F-Finlay.' Oliver

26

laughs. 'You'll need them. Oh, yeah, and ask for a miracle while you're at it. You're gonna need one of those to beat me, too.'

I clench my jaw and dig deep into the lettered tiles.

Oliver might have the upper hand when it comes to intimidating people, but I can still teach him a lesson in my own way.

Oliver plays S-K-I-N-T. Quick as a flash I play T-W and T around his I.

T-W-I-T.

I look at him.

He sticks his hand in the tile bag and glares back at me.

'You'll know all about what it feels like to be a massive twit,' he growls, placing his new tiles on the rack.

While I rummage around for three new letters, he plays I-N by the side of my T, making TIN. Three piddling points.

I smile and reach for the X on my rack. I place it above Oliver's I, straight on to a pale blue, double-word square. Eighteen tasty points for me.

'What the hell is that supposed to say?' he laughs out loud. '"Xi" isn't a word, you moron. Play again.'

I shake my head.

'You can't have those points, you stinking cheat,' he raises his voice. 'You can't just make up words.'

Mrs Adams strolls over, arms folded.

'What's the problem here?' She looks at the board and frowns.

'He's clueless, miss,' Oliver says. 'He can't even spell properly. "Xi" isn't a word; he can't claim eighteen points for that.'

'Actually, "xi" *is* a word, Oliver, it's the name of a Greek letter.' Mrs Adams smiles at me. 'One of the most popular two-letter words played in Scrabble, in fact.'

I smile back at her, just to get at Oliver.

'I've had enough of this stupid game,' Oliver snaps, throwing down the tile bag.

'Now, now, come on, Oliver,' Mrs Adams answers. 'Your Duke of Edinburgh Award is all about helping others.'

Oliver clenches his jaw and refuses to look at me while Mrs Adams stands and watches our next few turns.

Oliver plays T-U-R-N, C-L-A-S-P and B-O-O-K.

I play S-O-U-K, which is a Middle Eastern marketplace; add to existing letters to make V-E-N-T-R-O-U-S, meaning 'adventurous' – which gets me a score of sixty-five; and then, even though I have the letters to make up a higher-points word, I play T-H-U-G with a smirk in Oliver's direction, for the satisfying score of watching his face turn a deep crimson.

When the score reaches 358–179 in my favour, Oliver tips over his rack of letters, shoves his chair back and stalks off without saying a word.

One of the sixth-formers, a tall girl who is wearing a headscarf, looks over. She gives me a little, mischievous smile.

Mrs Adams shakes her head in disapproval as she watches Oliver leave.

'I think, Maryam, we have a little Scrabble dark horse here,' Mrs Adams says, looking at the girl and then back at me.

'I think you might be right, Mrs Adams,' the girl replies.

Mrs Adams bends down closer to me.

'So, Finlay, are you ready for your next challenge?'

I look back at her.

'Wh-wh—'

'Is that a yes? I *am* pleased.'

'Wh-wh-what –'

'What is it? Well, your challenge is to play Maryam, in here tomorrow lunchtime.' Mrs Adams grins and switches to a loud theatrical whisper behind her hand, as though Maryam can't hear. 'Don't tell anyone but Maryam used to be a member of the Pakistani Youth Scrabble Team.'

I look at Maryam. Tiny black sparkles twinkle at me from the edge of her headscarf.

I'm not joining the Scrabble club, not after today's performance with Oliver. But playing someone really good like Maryam might be fun, not that I'd have a chance of winning. It'd make a change from sitting on my own outside the PE store waiting for the afternoon bell to sound, anyway.

'Interested?' Mrs Adams asks.

I nod.

'Excellent. See you here at twelve thirty tomorrow, then,' Mrs Adams says, just as a text from Dad arrives to say he's outside.

BLANK TILES HAVE ZERO VALUE.

When I jump into the van, Dad turns off his *Best of the Eighties* playlist, which usually means he wants to talk.

The rain has stopped so I open the window a bit and kick an empty fag packet away from my foot.

'I've got to spend some time away from home, Finlay,' Dad says. He stares straight ahead at the road and his face looks more serious than usual. 'It'll just be for two or three nights a week.'

I feel the letters and words begin to clog up in my mouth, even though I don't know what it is I want to say yet.

'I don't like leaving you to your own devices, you know that, don't you? But this job, it's going to pay really well.' He glances at me then. 'You gonna be OK, pal?'

I nod.

'It'll mean you getting home from school a few days a week under your own steam, mind.'

'Th-that's f-fine,' I say.

I'd rather face Oliver than have the whole school thinking I'm a big kid who has to wait for his daddy to pick him up every night after school.

'You're a big lad now, fourteen going on forty-four, at times. More sensible than I ever was at your age. You must take after . . .'

His words tail off.

I look at him.

'Well, you're more sensible than I was, is all I meant to say.'

We never talk about Mum but she's there all the time, anyway. She exists in the silences between our words.

'I-I'll be al-al-all right,' I manage.

Dad looks at me as though he's trying to weigh up if I'm telling him the truth but he doesn't say anything.

With the music off, I can hear the growl of the diesel engine and the squeaky brakes. I'd like to tell Dad about the school Scrabble club but the amount of effort it's going to take to get the words out makes my insides feel all tight. I decide to try anyway.

'I pl-played Sc-Sc-Scr—' It just won't come.

'Scrabble?' Dad offers.

I nod.

'J-just n-now, in the sc-school l-library.'

'That's nice,' he says, pulling on the handbrake when we stop at a red light. He taps his fingers on the steering wheel as if the eighties soundtrack is still playing in his head.

'Don't know what you see in board games myself, mind. At your age, I was out playing footy every night.' His eyes roll up to inspect the sky for signs of rain. 'Nice weather for it, this. Playing footy, I mean.'

I haven't told him about playing Maryam tomorrow lunchtime yet. I can feel the sentences stacking up on top of my tongue like a Jenga-style word tower.

When I open my mouth to speak, it feels like all the letters will spill out like sharp little splinters until none of them make any sense at all.

It's easier to just keep quiet.

When we get home, Dad tells me all about the new job while we eat tea. He's got to travel down south to Brighton and stay overnight. He's won the joinery contract on some new high-end houses in a gated complex close to the sea.

'This could be the making of us, son,' Dad says, shovelling in half a sausage doused in ketchup. 'If I impress this building company, there'll be no more egg and beans for tea, I promise you that. It'll be champagne and caviar all the way.'

Sounds promising, but I know that chips, egg and beans happens to be Dad's favourite meal of all time. He even asked for it at the posh afternoon tea he treated

Mum to for their fifteenth wedding anniversary. I doubt he'd trade it in for all the champagne and caviar in the world.

Then I remember I haven't told Dad about Alex yet.

'I me-met a new b-boy –'

'At school? That's good, you need more friends, Finlay. When I was your age I had dozens of mates. We all hung around together down the park after school. My mate, Pete, says his lad is never in the house, and I got to thinking about you, spending half your life upstairs in your bedroom, peddling daft word games online.'

Dad swallows his food and actually puts down his fork.

'Look, I know it must be hard making friends. Not being able to talk properly and all that, it's a terrible shame when you think about it.' Dad smiles encouragingly at me. 'Tell you what, if this job comes good, I can send you to a specialist medical place to help sort you out. What do you say to that?'

My face burns.

Dad hardly ever mentions my stutter; I know he feels ashamed of it as much as I do. He's always sworn that, left alone, the problem will sort itself out. So I know it's a big thing for him to offer to send me somewhere.

Trouble is, I don't want to go to a *specialist medical place* and get forced to speak by 'some jumped-up know-it-all therapist', which is what Dad usually says about those sorts of people.

I'd rather keep quiet, and that way, it might not get noticed as much.

'Th-thanks Dad, b-but –'

'Good, that's settled then.' Dad beams, picking up his fork again. 'Now then, how does tinned fruit and ice cream sound for pudding?'

THE FIRST STAGE OF PLAY IS FOR EACH PLAYER TO BLINDLY SELECT ONE TILE FROM THE BAG.

While Dad's getting ready to go back out on a job, I stack our dirty plates and dishes in the sink.

'I shouldn't be too long,' Dad says, walking into the room and shrugging on his heavy wool jacket. 'I've got floorboards to replace in a council house in St Ann's and then it's Mrs Taylor's back gate again. God knows when she'll see fit to replace the bloody thing.'

Mrs Taylor's husband died ten years ago and left her very comfortably off.

'That woman's allergic to replacing anything,' Dad bellows from the bottom of the stairs as he laces his boots. 'I keep telling her, she could have bought a fancy new wrought iron gate with the money it's taking to keep paying me to repair the old one.'

I wouldn't say Dad is a good businessman. He's always advising his customers how to save money and stop calling him out as much. Mum was much sharper. She started her own IT consultancy a year before she left and it was doing really well, too. She'd won a contract with a big IT company in the area.

She worked really hard, and for what?

After she left, Dad found out she'd wound up her business. It was just another thing that didn't make any sense.

Back in my bedroom when Dad's gone, my skin feels itchy and my legs are restless.

Once I start thinking about Mum, it's hard to stop.

Neville isn't out yet so I can't talk to him.

I upend the tile bag on to the big square board of wood that Dad gave me for my anagram practice.

I like the tinkling sound as the tiles tumble out. The hard black letters on the soft cream-coloured plastic feel solid when I run my fingers over them. I turn over each of the ninety-eight tiles so the letters are face up and set the two blank tiles aside. I select six letters and set out the word in front of me:

VETOED

I slide the letters around and make a note of all the words I can find in it, on my anagram pad:

DEVOTE, VOTE, TEED, DOVE, DOTE, VETO

I won't go to a clinic, as Dad has suggested. I'd much rather just speak less until the stutter goes away. I've got some other tricks I can use, too. Sometimes, I can avoid the words I stutter on the most and choose easier words to say.

The letter tiles stay exactly where I put them on the wooden slate. They don't morph into different words that other people can't understand.

My heart stops thumping so hard and the itchy feeling eases off.

I push VETOED away and turn to a fresh page in my notebook. I set out a new word.

DISEASE

SEASIDE, EASES, IDEAS, SEISE, ASIDES, SAID

I don't want to be known as the boy who stutters. I wish I could reinvent myself as a normal lad who doesn't get noticed in class. The sort of lad a mum would never want to leave.

I select seven new letters and try to concentrate. I can make the stutter go away, it just takes time. Talking about it with some know-all therapist is the last thing I need.

I glance at the clock; 6.30. My Scrabble group should all be online now.

I flick a switch and the computer blinks into life. I grab handfuls of tiles and put them back in the bag and when I look up, I have a message box flashing.

Hi Finlay, fancy a game? A ☺

It's almost as though Alex has been waiting for me to log on. This is what it must feel like to have a good friend.

Hi Alex, ready to go when you are.

I need to tell him about the no-chatting rule but I can do that later.

My turn first. The virtual tiles have given me T-V-E-P-S-A-L.

I click my first word into play in the middle of the board.

P-A-V-E-S [10]

You had a good day? he asks.

Somehow, I don't feel as irritated by his chat as I did before. I'm almost looking forward to telling Alex about my day – the bits I want him to know, that is. I can reinvent myself and he'll never know.

Not bad. You? I type.

Crap day at school, double maths.

Tough, I send back. **Went to Scrabble after-sch club first time, today.**

Cool. You win??

Yeah, playing ex-champ tomoro lunchtime.

You'll smash it!

The dark cloud that has hovered above my head since the therapist conversation with Dad has finally drifted away.

It feels great to have someone around that's interested in what you're up to.

Alex plays V-A-P-I-D off my V and collects eleven points.

Good one, I say.

Uh-oh, problem here, back in 2 mins.

I study my online letter rack, wondering what's

happening Alex's end. Finally, I decide on P-R-I-N-T, leading off Alex's P and picking up a double-word square.

It's been six minutes now and there's still no response from Alex.

Hope everything is OK, I tap into the message box.

Nothing for another fifty-one seconds and then he's back.

Sorry about that. Parent trouble.

You OK? I don't know what else to say.

Yeah, you know how it is. They're arguing. AGAIN.

I remember that melting feeling inside when Mum and Dad fought. It got worse just before she left, they argued louder and more often.

I decide not to comment and just wait for Alex to play his turn.

Don't know why Dad puts up with Stepmum, she can be such a bitch.

Strong words. I send a sad face emoticon because I can't think of anything else to say.

What he says next sets my heart hammering, my mouth dries out in an instant.

Get this. She walked out on her own family a couple of years back without even saying goodbye . . . I mean, how can you justify THAT?

THE TILE NEAREST TO 'A' WINS AND
THAT PLAYER EARNS THE FIRST TURN.

Thursday

It's two in the morning and for some reason I've just snapped awake.

I can't get back to sleep, despite the fact I've got a big Scrabble game with Maryam scheduled for later.

There's this rotten trick that life likes playing on you, when you've something important to do the next day. The more you tell yourself you've got to get some sleep, the more awake your brain gets. Scientists say it's all to do with low melatonin levels, whatever they are, but I reckon it's to do with worries, plain and simple.

I'm churning inside, asking questions and demanding answers where there aren't any. When Alex said his stepmum had left her family, I didn't say a single thing. I just turned off the computer and sat staring at my bedroom wall for ages.

Because that's exactly what Mum did to me and Dad, two years ago.

Later, I logged back on, thinking maybe I could find out more. But Alex wasn't there.

'I don't believe in coincidences,' Mum always used to say.

But here is a big fat coincidence, involving someone just like Mum or . . . my breath catches in my throat . . . someone who could even *be* Mum.

What if Alex's stepmum and my mum are *one and the same person*?

I know it's mad. And yet I can't seem to get it out of my head.

I throw off the quilt, sit up in bed and look through the gap in my curtains. The sodium-orange glow of the next street's lamp-posts lights up my room.

After pushing Mum to the back of my mind for all this time, the thought that she might be closer than I think turns my insides into a mixed up *mojito* – those bitter-sweet cocktails she used to drink.

I cover my face with my hands as if that can stop the thoughts. Two days ago I didn't even *know* Alex, and now I've virtually convinced myself he lives with *my mum*. They'll be carting me off to the doctor if I let on what I'm thinking.

I take a deep breath and let it out slowly. It's been such a long time since I've had a good friend. Back in my old school, me and my mates were round at each other's houses all the time.

When me and Dad moved, we all said that somehow we'd find a way to still meet up regularly, that we wouldn't lose touch. But twelve miles is a long way to go when you're just twelve years old.

Looking back, it was never going to work out.

I don't want anything to spoil my chance of making friends with Alex, especially something that's just in my imagination. You know if you're going get along with people when you first meet them. It's just a feeling, but I know that me and Alex have what it takes to be good mates.

The rattling starts and minuscule shavings of wood begin flying around the carpet. Neville is going loopy, whizzing round on his wheel like a mad thing. I can smell the fresh sawdust I put in there yesterday. I creep over to him and sit next to his cage. His black, beady eyes glint in the gloom, like tiny buttons of polished jet.

Neville was a birthday present from Mum, she got him for me just a couple of months before she left home. I remember her coming into the living room to tell me and Dad she had read some research that said people's stammers sometimes disappeared when they talked to animals.

Dad said it was a load of old tosh and we both laughed. But when Neville came to live with us, I realized that everything Mum had said was true.

'Could it be her, Neville?' I whisper. 'Could it actually

b-be *my* mum who is living with Alex?'

Neville is too busy in his endless marathon-running task to even notice I'm there. He's wearing himself out, and for what? There's nothing at the end of it.

I creep downstairs for a glass of water and find Dad fast asleep in his chair.

I heard him come up to check on me last night when he got back home. Sometimes, I think he just likes to check I've not gone back to logging trains all night long.

I really wanted to talk to him about Mum and Alex but the words got wedged in my throat, so I pretended to be asleep. It was just easier that way.

I stand in front of his chair for a moment or two and watch as his broad chest rises and falls with each long breath. His thick, black hair flops over one eye and I spot tiny flecks of grey that I haven't noticed before.

Dad's face has softened in sleep. The two pinched creases in the middle of his eyebrows are relaxed now but his hands still grip the arms of his chair as if he's scared he might slip and fall.

When I was little, I used to climb on to his back.

He'd stalk around the house like a giant, searching for me, pretending he didn't know I was clinging on there. I remember the soft flannel of his checked shirt – it always smelt of wood, creosote and the sharp tang of varnish. It was a smell that made me feel safe.

If I bend closer to him now, he'll just stink of cigarette

smoke. He lights up the second he has a moment of spare time, as if he's trying to fill up an empty space in his chest.

Dad's work boots have faded to a sort of dark, sandy colour and the metal toecaps poke through the ragged leather like discoloured teeth. Clumps of site muck and hard earth are scattered on the carpet around his feet.

We moved house about a month after Mum left. Dad mumbled something about a smaller mortgage and bad memories and that was it, all decided. I left my mates and school. I was worried Mum would come back and wonder where we had gone.

'That's not going to happen,' Dad said angrily, when I told him.

After that, I stopped asking. I didn't even tell him about the bad dreams that started. I tried not to speak at all.

There were rules at our old house that used to get on my nerves.

No shoes on in the house.

Fresh vegetables or salad with every meal.

No fizzy pop because you've seen what it does to a coin dropped in a glass of it, so think what does it does to your stomach.

I wish I had those rules back now.

It all seems a long time ago now and I can't remember that much about meeting up with my mates on the field after school or pooling all our loose change to buy a big bag of chips to share.

Most of the time I don't want to remember.

I turn all the lights off, apart from the lamp in the hallway. But I don't wake Dad.

Thursday, 14 May
Dear Mum,

I know this is a bit heavy for 2.30 in the morning but I wanted to ask, do you think something still belongs to a person if they've left it behind?

I'm not the only kid around here who hasn't got a mum. There are kids at school whose mums have died and everyone feels really sorry about it. Although they aren't around any more, their mums still count.

In Computer Studies, some kids made Mother's Day cards using online TEMPLATES [13]. Even Evie Sanders made one, and her mum died last year in a car accident. Evie said she wanted to put the card on the grave with some pink roses, like her mum was still here to see it. Mr Cawthorne said it was a lovely sentiment and all her friends fussed round her and did that weird group-hug thing that girls do.

I thought about making you a card, I really wanted to. But I couldn't bring myself to say so to Mr Cawthorne, in the end. See, Mum, it makes a difference that you haven't died. It's like the rules no longer apply because you're *just gone*.

I've done everything I can think of, to find out where you are. I've googled every possible spelling of your name, married and maiden surnames, old addresses. I even rang the IT firm you used to work for, but I got nothing. If I were a twenty-five-year-old man, I might get a bit further. I could pay for a private investigator to help track you down or at least make enquiries with the people who knew you.

But soon as I speak to anyone on the phone, I just sound like a sad little kid that's trying to find his mum and nobody takes me seriously at all.

I've tried to talk to Dad about it but soon as I mention your name, it's like this heavy curtain comes down over his face. His features set into that same grim look, like when you two used to argue and you'd make him feel stupid with all your clever words.

A couple of months after we'd moved house, I holed myself up in my bedroom and wouldn't come downstairs at all. I'd been trying to make a video message for my old mates, but the words wouldn't come out right. Dad came in to try and talk me into coming down for tea and my webcam recorded our conversation. I've watched it so many times, when I close my eyes, it's like I can see it playing in my head:

'W-w-what if Mum n-needs our h-help?' I shout at him. 'W-what if s-s-s-something's happened to her, and she can't get b-back home? We can't just f-forget about her.'

'Trust me, Finlay, your mum is OK.'

'But h-how do you know that?' I yell. 'Have you heard from her and n-n-not told m-me?'

'No,' he says quietly. 'No, I haven't heard anything from

your mum. I give you my word that if I do, I will tell you.'

'Then h-how do you know she's OK?' I scowl at him. You can see me balling my hands into fists on the video. *'How do you know she's n-n-not waiting for us to f-find her?'*

If you watch closely, you can see a CHINK [14] appear in Dad's 'face curtain'. But what it reveals isn't light or hope. It is the blackest darkness, like when there's been a power cut and not a single glint of light is left.

Dad says, *'I know your mum's OK because she took her name off our joint bank account. She cancelled her running magazine subscription and she even told the lady who takes her yoga class she wouldn't be coming any more. She changed the parental contact details at your school into my name only.'* Dad grasps my shoulders and looks at me, his eyes dark and shining. *'That's how I know, Finlay. She doesn't want to be found.'*

You told everyone who mattered you were going, Mum. Except for me and Dad. You didn't tell us anything at all.

There has to be a reason, an explanation. People like you don't just disappear.

Do you still think of me as your son if you chose to leave me behind? Or have you forgotten me already?

I don't think I will ever forget you.

Love,

Finlay x

A PLAYER WILL WIN FIRST TURN OUTRIGHT IF THEY SELECT A BLANK TILE.

Later that morning when I get to school, Mrs Adams pokes her head out of the library doors as I walk past.

'Now, Finlay, don't go forgetting about your Scrabble game with Maryam this lunchtime.' She speaks slowly, like I might have a problem understanding. 'Afterwards, we can have a chat about the game and Maryam might even give you some tips on how to improve.' Her voice follows me down the corridor.

I turn and give a little nod, swallowing down a sickly taste.

Speaking to Maryam means forcing words out, like pushing crusty old toothpaste through a bunged-up tube.

First, there's double Maths to get through but I don't mind that. Numbers are practical and straightforward, and best of all, it's a subject where hardly any talking is needed.

In Scrabble, it doesn't matter if you know the meaning

of a word, it's the *score* that is more important to the game.

Mr Trevor asks for volunteers to solve the equation on the whiteboard.

Predictably, there is silence.

'Finlay, we haven't had the benefit of your maths expertise for a while, why don't you have a crack at it?'

My heart slumps into my shoes. A few teachers think that speaking in front of everyone will help cure a stammer. Mr Trevor is one of them.

A flash of laughter erupts from the back row.

'Is it f-four, Finlay? Or maybe it's f-fifty-f-five.'

I press my palms into the desk but my hands still shake.

'Oliver,' Mr Trevor bellows, 'if you're feeling cleverer than usual this morning, perhaps you'd like to provide us all with the correct solution?'

The laughter dies down.

'Come up to the front, Finlay.' He's all upbeat and jolly. 'You can tell us the answer and then pop it on the whiteboard so we can all see it.'

My face feels hot when I stand up. Maybe I can get through this without saying anything at all.

Not everyone needs words to get stuff said. There's this actual whistling language called Yupik that Inuits in Alaska still use. Words get lost across massive mountain ranges and crazy-steep canyons. The best way to talk to other people over long distances is by whistling.

Children who speak Yupik learn to whistle their own names. I wonder what *Finlay* would sound like? If I knew, I could whistle it instead of juddering through all those false starts before my name finally pops out. I could even whistle my maths answer to Mr Trevor right now.

Something small and hard hits the back of my head as I walk over to the whiteboard. An eraser bounces off into the corner of the classroom.

Silently I solve the equation and write the answer on to the board. I can see Mr Trevor's mouth moving but he sounds as if he is underwater. I wipe my clammy hands on my trousers and try to breathe normally when I walk back to my seat. It feels like I'm in one of those dreams where you need to run fast but you can only walk like an astronaut.

There are snorts of laughter from the front row behind me and I can see Oliver in the back row ahead of me. His mouth is in the 'F-F-Finlay' shape but blood is rushing in my ears and I can't tell exactly what he is saying.

Then Mr Trevor claps his hands and the sounds around me become crystal clear again.

'*Calm down,*' Mr Trevor's voice booms, 'or you'll all be staying in at break.'

I purse my lips and pretend I'm whistling in Yupik. I blow out the air but I don't actually make a sound, not a whisper. *Oliver Haywood, you are a sad, ugly loser.* I could whistle that right in his face if I were an Inuit and he'd never even know what it means.

When the bell rings at the end of the second Maths session, I sit on the little patch of scrubby grass behind the Science Block and read through my anagram notebook, just for something to do until it's time to go to the library.

I hardly ever go into the *bull ring*, as I call the dining hall.

Once, my parents had been arguing for about a week over something. I could hear them even though they always closed the kitchen door. After that, Dad booked a surprise long weekend to Seville in Spain for Mum's birthday.

Seville is a beautiful city but they haven't banned bullfighting, like Barcelona has.

The tour guide took us to a bull ring and told us how they drugged the bulls so all the odds were stacked against the animal.

'People can be horribly cruel, Finlay,' Mum said. 'Never forget that.'

In the dining hall, I am one of those bulls. I even feel drugged.

It doesn't matter if you sit quietly in a corner minding your own business or near the lunchtime supervisors, someone always starts prodding you for a reaction.

I pull a small plastic bag out of my rucksack. There wasn't much in the house to bring for lunch, so today it's just a slice of bread and jam, an apple and an out-of-date yogurt.

With Dad rushing about so much, he sometimes just forgets to get anything in apart from stuff for tea on the way home, but today it doesn't matter because I'm not hungry at all.

I feel a bit nervous, which is silly.

I'm starting to wonder why I agreed to play Scrabble with Maryam in the first place. She used to play for Pakistan, she's going to turn me into pizza topping.

By the time I reach the library doors, I've convinced myself that the whole thing is a really bad idea. My throat feels dry and tight, as if the words are already lining up in there, ready to spill out in a stammer-fit the second I open my mouth.

You don't have to do this.

It's that voice in my head that encourages me to stay silent because it knows what an idiot I make of myself. Today, I think the voice is correct. I really don't have to put myself through this: I can just say I forgot about the game.

I manage to take just three steps in the other direction when the library doors whoosh open behind me.

'Finlay, you're right on time,' Mrs Adams calls and steps out into the corridor. 'I've been looking forward to this all morning.'

She propels me back around and we walk into the library together.

All morning, I've imagined the entire Scrabble club, including Oliver Haywood, gathered like a small mob around the table where Maryam and I will play like bugs under a microscope.

But when I get inside the library, nobody is in there at all, apart from Mrs Adams and Maryam.

'We're closing the library for half an hour this lunchtime so you and Maryam get to play in peace.' Mrs Adams smiles and bustles back towards her office. 'That OK with you, Finlay?'

'Th-th—'

'You're very welcome. Would you like a glass of water?'

'Pl, pl—'

'Consider it done.'

I bite down on my tongue.

Maryam steals a glance at me, rolls her eyes and grins.

THE FIRST WORD MUST BE PLACED IN THE CENTRE OF THE BOARD AND UTILIZE THE 'STAR' SQUARE.

Everything is laid out on a small table ready for play. There's the Scrabble board, set on a proper turntable, a tile bag and even a professional-looking digital timer.

Mrs Adams comes back with two glasses of water.

The strip light above us lights up the board so it is stark and bright. Everything feels out in the open.

Maryam sits down and I shrug off my blazer and hang it over the back of my chair.

'Anything else you need, Finlay?' Mrs Adams asks.

I don't want to speak and look stupid but there *is* something else I need.

Maryam leans back in her chair, watching me.

'C-could we use m-my, m-my –'

Try as I might, I can't get past the simple word 'my'.

Maryam stares, like she's only just seeing me for the first time.

'Would you like to write it down, Finlay?' Mrs Adams asks.

I shake my head.

'Spell it out in Scrabble tiles?'

I squeeze my eyes shut. Tiny beads of sweat bubble across my upper lip.

'C-could we use m-my t-tile b-bag?' I manage eventually.

'Of course,' Mrs Adams says. 'No problem at all.'

She scurries off to fetch something.

I slip Mum's tile bag from my rucksack. The muted tinkle of the tiles on the board sounds like whispered secrets.

'How long have you had a stammer?' Maryam asks softly.

People usually snigger or whisper behind my back. Nobody ever asks me anything directly about my stutter.

My face feels hot and I look away but she waits for an answer.

'F-f-forever,' I say, because that's what it feels like.

I used to think I had a bit of a stammer before Mum left, but I realize it was nothing, compared to now.

Maryam wins the draw and begins the game with V-E-X-E-D, using a blank tile for the X and earning her a very respectable thirty-two points.

My heart begins to thump faster as I study my tiles and realize an explosive way to use one of Maryam's E's. I add two of my letters above and below it, to make H-E-X, scoring twenty-five points because I use two double-letter squares.

'I'm impressed,' Maryam says.

I catch movement from the corner of my eye and lose concentration for a moment as my body floods with dread at the prospect of Oliver barging in on our game, but it's just Mrs Adams, edging closer to watch.

My heart sinks when I pull a J as one of my tiles, but when Maryam plays K-I-T-E for nine points, I'm able to use the J on my next turn, playing J-A-C-K-S and taking in a double-word square for a tasty thirty-six points.

A couple of turns later, Maryam hits back with Q-U-I-P-S, earning forty-eight points by using a triple-letter square.

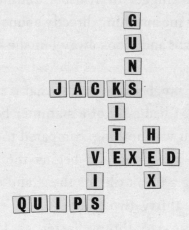

One of us lands a good, hard jab and then a couple of turns later, the other one recovers and comes back with a left hook.

Seventeen minutes in, the score is 172–149 to Maryam.

For the next couple of turns, Maryam continues to pull slowly ahead. When I glance at the clock again, I realize we have just two minutes of play left and the score is now 211–179 to her.

'You get the last turn, Finlay.' She smiles.

I nod and stick my hand into the tile bag. I don't mind losing, Maryam is obviously a much better player than me. And then I land the Z.

As I place it on my tile rack and begin to fiddle around with my letters to see what I can get, the realization hits me. My anagram training kicks in and the nonsensical mix on my rack suddenly reads B-A-Z-O-O-K-A.

I transfer all seven of my letters on to the board.

'Bingo,' Mrs Adams gasps. 'You got a Bingo!'

I utilize Maryam's S and a triple-word square and B-A-Z-O-O-K-A-S earns me 119 points.

Mrs Adams chalks up the final score: 211–298. To me.

THE 'STAR' SQUARE IN THE MIDDLE OF THE BOARD EARNS THE FIRST PLAYER A DOUBLE-WORD SCORE.

Maryam reaches over to shake my hand. 'A brilliant finish. Congratulations.'

'Very well done, Finlay,' Mrs Adams drawls, like I'm a three-year-old. She pulls up a chair. 'I feel a little silly now, assuming you didn't know how to play the game yesterday.'

Maryam starts to bend the board into a funnel shape and all the tiles tumble into a long, narrow pile.

'Y-you haven't t-taken a ph-photograph,' I say, even though it's too late to do anything about it now.

'A photograph?' Maryam's eyebrows knit together.

'Of th-the b-board.'

'That's not common practice, apart from championship games,' Mrs Adams says.

A couple of weeks before she left, Mum took a photograph of every single one of our finished games.

Maybe she meant to take them with her for memory's sake but I found them in an envelope in my desk drawer.

I shrug and reach for the tile bag.

'So, you are not a member of a Scrabble club, Finlay?' Maryam asks.

'N-no,' I say. 'I p-play on-on—'

'Online,' Mrs Adams says, stretching out the word. 'He plays online.'

When people finish my sentences, the flow of words sometimes seizes up completely. I can't really blame people for doing it, they're bound to get fed up of waiting.

I watch all the letters mix and tangle into one big mess as they fall into the bag.

'There's no substitute for the excitement of playing one to one,' Mrs Adams comments.

I'm not going to join the after-school club, if that's what she's hinting at.

We all look up as someone raps on the library-door glass. My heart begins to bump against my chest, like it's trying to burst out.

'Ah, excellent timing.' Mrs Adams beams as she gets up.

A face presses against the glass and I suddenly feel very sick.

'Come in, Oliver.' She unlocks the library door and Oliver slouches in, leaving Darren and Mitchell waiting outside.

'I didn't know there was a lunchtime club on today.' Oliver glares over at me.

'There isn't,' Mrs Adams says lightly. 'But I'm glad you dropped by, Oliver. I have a little proposal for both you . . . and Finlay.' She looks at Maryam.

I catch my breath before it chokes me.

Please don't ask me to partner up with Oliver, I silently repeat in my head.

'How would you boys feel about getting some extra coaching in, with a view to entering the National School Scrabble Championships?' Mrs Adam's face lights up. 'You'd get to represent the school.'

There's a weird mix of excitement and dread sloshing around in my stomach.

'I thought you said *I* was going to be the one representing the school.' Oliver folds his arms in a huff.

'Well, if you cast your mind back, what I actually said is that you were definitely in with a *chance*, Oliver.' Mrs Adams has got this habit of closing her eyes when she speaks and her eyelids flicker like she's having a bad dream. 'If the school puts two players forward, that will increase our chance of success.'

'I'm not playing with *him*,' Oliver says sulkily. 'He can't even speak properly.'

'There's no need for that.' Mrs Adams's voice sharpens.

Entering the championship might mean I'll have to actually *talk* to people. I'll have to say my name and school at the very least . . . in front of *crowds* of people.

I loosen my tie and hold my collar away from my neck to get a bit of air in.

'Maryam has very kindly agreed to coach both of you,' Mrs Adams says.

'How come *she's* not entering if she's so good?' Oliver says slyly.

'I played competitively for three years in Pakistan,' Maryam replies. 'But it was my uncle's dream, I am afraid, not mine. But I am very happy to help you both to improve your game.'

'That's very good of you.' Oliver narrows his eyes at Maryam. 'But I don't think there's that much I could learn from *you*.'

Mrs Adams frowns and leans forward, pinning me to the spot with her magnified eyes.

'What about you, Finlay? I've been waiting for a budding champion to walk into this library for years and now I'm lucky enough to have two very good players in you and Oliver.'

'I d-don—'

'You do? That's splendid. Maryam will organize . . .'

I shake my head and look away from her.

'It's OK, Finlay,' Maryam says. 'You don't have to decide now.'

Oliver grins.

'Look, take some time,' Mrs Adams says. 'You can

come and see me any time if you have any questions about the process.'

She looks so hopeful.

'I d-don't kn-know if I w-want to,' I say at last.

'He's shaking like a leaf.' Oliver sniggers. 'How is he going to manage to play a game under pressure?'

'Oliver.' Mrs Adams sighs. 'If you're not interested in extra coaching and you're here to try and undermine a fellow student, then you might as well leave right now.'

Oliver stares at his feet.

'I'll review the situation in a week's time when we'll have a play-off in the library. I can't say any fairer than that.' Mrs Adams peers down at Oliver through her spectacles. 'Unless you've changed your mind and you *want* to take the extra training with Maryam?'

Oliver smirks and shakes his head.

'Next week I'll make a decision about who will represent the school and who will be the substitute,' Mrs Adams says. 'You'll both get to take part in the championships, either way.'

'I'm the best,' Oliver says as he starts to walk away. 'We all know that.'

Mrs Adams shakes her head and sighs as she watches Oliver leave but she doesn't say anything. For all of three seconds. 'I'm pleased you're going to take up the offer of extra training, Finlay,' she witters. 'I can clear a space for you in here most lunchtimes. And at weekends, I'm sure that my colleague at the youth club will be happy to provide a place for you and Maryam to use for training purposes.'

I think about confessing my worries about speaking at the championships as a reason for pulling out.

But then Mrs Adams says something that changes everything.

'Of course, if you won a national title at such a young age, you'd create a media frenzy, Finlay. Everybody, all over the country would see what you'd achieved.'

Everybody. All over the country.

Although I've never wanted to be famous, or rich, or anything else lots of people at school seem to want to be, I suddenly realize that taking part in the championships could give me the one thing I want most in the world.

To make my mum proud.

I don't know if or when I'll get to see her again, but *what if?*

What if I *do* find Mum? What if (even though a big part of me thinks it's totally crazy and I'm mad for even thinking it) she *does* live with Alex and his dad?

I'd want her to be proud of me. I'd want her to see that although words have beaten me in one way, I've conquered them in another.

Even if Mum *doesn't* live with Alex, winning the championships could give me a way to finally make contact with her. Wherever she is now, there'd be a brilliant chance that she'd see my photograph if it was plastered all over the newspapers and possibly even on the TV.

A warm feeling channels down my arms and legs. Suddenly, I feel unstoppable.

'I'll d-do it,' I say.

SUBSEQUENT WORDS PLAYED
WILL BRANCH OUT ON TO
SURROUNDING SQUARES.

The afternoon lessons pass in a bit of blur.

Miss Poole's History lesson starts in 1831 in Ohio at the beginning of the travels of the Mormons. Five minutes before the end of class we're in 1847, the Mormons have reached the Great Salt Lake and I've barely heard any of it.

I'm worried Alex might not make contact again. He might be fed up because I just cut him off last night.

When the final bell rings at the end of the afternoon, I pile into the corridor with everyone else and let the crowd-swell carry me to the main doors.

Someone thumps me hard in the back and sends me crashing into a girl.

'S-sorry,' I say. When she turns around, I see it's Maryam.

She shakes her head in disgust at someone behind me.

'What're you looking at?' Oliver snaps at her. 'Why are you even in our country?'

I twist around and find he's so close I can smell his sour breath.

'I suppose you think you're the Scrabble king now, you loser,' he growls in my ear. 'As if *you're* good enough to play in the championships.'

'Yeah, it's Oliver who was supposed to be the one going to the championships, you moron,' his mate Darren calls out.

'Shut it, you idiot,' Oliver snaps at him, his eyes darting around to see if anyone heard. 'I wasn't even bothered about going, anyway.'

Hot, clumsy bodies push and pull all around me. I feel a bit dizzy and turn back around but Oliver barges past, so now he's in front of me.

'You do realize you have to make a speech if you win, right?' He laughs. 'You'll have to thank people and stuff. But you can't even say your own flipping name, you loser. You're gonna be such a laughing-stock, I can't wait.'

I open my mouth but nothing comes out.

'S-see y-ya, don't wanna b-be ya!' Oliver laughs and drops back to join his mates.

I look for Maryam to ask her if she's OK, but she has disappeared into the crowd.

I loiter around the side of the building until I can see that Oliver and his mates are safely on the bus. Dad is only five minutes late.

When I climb into the van, he's on a hands-free call, chatting to some bloke about the job in Brighton and he stays on the phone for most of the journey.

The van motors through the traffic and I stare blankly out of the window. When I think about speaking in front of lots of people at the championships, my chest feels all tight. I imagine standing at the front of a room packed with people who are belly-laughing at my pathetic efforts to spit out a few mangled words. In the front row, Oliver and his mates point and yell, telling everyone what a loser I am.

The van turns into the next street and we drive slowly past my old primary school. Mum used to pick me up from here when I was younger. We'd walk home together, call for ice creams in the summer and kick dry orange and yellow leaves at each other in the autumn.

I feel the tightness in my chest loosen off a bit.

National Scrabble Champion. I can imagine that newspaper headline, complete with my photograph so Mum is in no doubt it's me.

Maybe she'll see it at breakfast time, when she's alone in a kitchen that looks just like ours used to be. Her eyes pop – her face lights up. A hand flies to her mouth. She's been searching everywhere and she's found me at last!

'Bloody hell, Finlay, snap out of it!' Dad bangs the steering wheel, making me jump. 'Three times I've asked you now.'

The van has stopped outside the Co-op.

'S-sorry,' I say.

'Well, which is it? Sausage, or fish fingers with your chips and beans?'

I'm not even hungry.

'F-fi—'

'Fish fingers it is then.' Dad jumps out of the van.

I try to go back to the comforting pictures of Mum but they've lost all their colour.

Now, all the images in my head just look flat and unreal.

WORDS CAN SPREAD OUT FROM
THE INITIAL WORD PLAYED,
IN ANY DIRECTION.

After we've had tea, I leave Dad making a list of what he needs to take with him to Brighton tomorrow, and I shoot upstairs to my room.

A second after I log in, the message box pops up.

Fancy a game? A

My stomach is churning with relief, but also with nerves. How I can get Alex talking about his stepmum again without it looking obvious?

There's so much at stake.

Sorry I broke off early yesterday . . . had the runs!! I type.

I don't know where the fib came from, but it sounds convincing.

Bad luck, he replies.

Usually, I'd want to stop the chatter and get on with the game but I need to keep Alex talking without raising his suspicions.

Just remembered you had trouble last night . . .

71

you OK? Your stepmum OK?

Yeah, everything's blown over, he says.

Think. Think. What else can I say about it?

Your stepmum sounds a bit moody.

I need him to talk about her.

Yeah, she can be. Your mum the same?

Now what do I say? *My mum left her family too, like your stepmum?* Or I could say: *Actually, I think your stepmum could be* my *mum.*

Not my best idea, it could scare Alex off. I really want to find out more about who he lives with but I don't want him to get tired of me asking questions. I'd like us to be friends.

My mum is away atm, I type. **With work.**

Quick as a flash he comes back.

What does she do?

She has her own IT company.

Cool! What's it called? Alex comes back quickly.

This is turning into a big fat spiderweb of lies.

She doesn't like me giving out her details online. Soz, I write back.

I wait for Alex to enter his first word on the board but nothing happens.

My dad is in IT, he says. **I'm a bit of a computer whizz, too!**

I'm pleased we've moved away from the subject of Mum now, I've got a chance to find out a bit more about Alex himself.

The back door slams and I hear Dad call goodbye as he leaves the house to do a couple of local jobs.

Cool. My dad has his own joinery business.

I travel with my dad during sch hols, Alex says. **He works in Manchester, London, Nottingham & Glasgow. You anywhere near any of those places?**

He comes to Nottingham. *He comes to Nottingham!*

I imagine meeting up with Alex, going bowling or to the cinema. We could even play Scrabble, here at my house. And then I remember that he doesn't know the real me. He doesn't know about my stutter.

Let's get the game started, I type, hoping Alex doesn't notice that I haven't answered his question.

We're ten minutes into the game but I can tell that Alex's heart isn't in it.

He's coming up with really short words that have tiny scores, as if he's putting no effort at all into playing. I don't want to decimate him by playing up to standard. That's not what friends do to each other.

So, do you get to speak to your mum when she's working away? he types.

This isn't the way it's supposed to go. I want to find out information about *his* family, not the other way round.

I try to think of an answer that's not an outright lie. It's difficult.

She rings or emails if she can. Haven't heard from her much this time.

Why's that?

Dunno, just haven't spoke to her for a while.

Before he can reply, I type again.

What does your stepmum do for a job?

A short pause, then:

She's like your mum . . . doesn't like me talking about it online.

I suppose I asked for that one.

We finish the game and Alex says he hasn't got time for another so we say our goodbyes and he logs off.

I look around. I can feel the silence of the house pressing up against my bedroom door. Dad will be out for ages but I hear a couple of scratches from Neville's cage.

I wait a few minutes but he doesn't poke his head out to say hello.

Thursday, 14 May
Dear Mum,

When I close my eyes to go to sleep, I go through this daft routine in my mind where I run through the reasons you might have left.

I don't know why I do it but it started the first night you'd gone and I've just kept going with it.

Some of the reasons are:

- *Someone ABDUCTED [14] you.* Obviously I don't like this one because you might've got hurt, but in a way it's my favourite, because it means you hadn't got a choice but to go.
- *You lost your memory.* Maybe you went somewhere up north or down south like you'd been doing those last few months, for an important meeting. You lost your memory and you still don't remember anything about who you are or where you came from. *After two years?* It could still be possible, I guess. If I ignore the fact that Dad said you'd planned to go.
- *You got lost.* Yeah, I know. Getting lost in the UK for two whole years isn't really possible.

But that's the best thing about my reason-for-leaving routine: anything counts and anything is considered. I'm still thinking of reasons. And now Alex has planted a new reason in my head that I don't like one bit.

• *You left to start a new family, somewhere else.*

I know this sort of thing happens. But it's the kind of thing I thought only happens to *other people*. Could it really be possible that I've met your *new* stepson online?

Surely, that wouldn't be so much a coincidence as a miracle.

Some nights, I pray that I'll have a dream which reveals the truth about what really happened to you – or at least gives me a clue. Anything.

And I pray hard that one day, you'll come back.

But now I'm starting to realize that hoping you'll come back is pointless, because even when I do dream about you, nothing ever works out the way I want it to.

In my dreams, you just pick up your handbag and suitcase and walk out the door without looking back. And the reason is obvious. It's always the same.

You just don't want us any more.

Love,

Finlay x

PLAYERS TAKE THEIR TURNS IN
A CLOCKWISE DIRECTION.

Friday

Definition of a good morning at school = keeping out of
Oliver's way. So I suppose you could say I had a good
morning.

At lunchtime I went straight to the library for my
first training session with Maryam. It felt great having
somewhere to go instead of sitting round the back of the
Science Block or outside the PE store, waiting for the bell
to go.

Sixth-formers can wear what they like but Maryam
is dressed in school uniform and wears a black headscarf
with sparkly silver dots all over it.

Her skin is smooth and pale brown and her eyes are
dark and glitter with something that looks like a cross
between amusement and mischief.

'Hey!' She plonks herself down at the table that Mrs
Adams has set up for us in a quiet corner of the library.
'Been looking forward to this, have you?'

Maryam's English is excellent. Her accent sounds

strong and proud and the way it mixes in with the local slang she's picked up is addictive to listen to.

'You don't have to do extra training, you know, if you don't want to. But Mrs Adams has got her hopes firmly pinned on you and Oliver.'

I shift around in my seat.

'Lucky Finlay, eh?' She sticks out her tongue and grins.

Maryam is not what I expected. At all.

From a distance she seems shy, aloof, even. She wasn't *this* chatty in front of Mrs Adams.

'Don't say much, do you?' She pulls a face. 'If I had a stammer, I'd still want to be heard.'

I look at her.

'I mean, if your eyesight was not so good, you would still look at the world around you, yes?'

She's being very direct and I'm being very quiet. There's a feeling in my chest like when I bolt my food down too fast.

'No matter if you ignore me, I am used to it,' she shrugs. 'Nobody wants to talk to the headscarf girl around here.'

I don't want Maryam to think I'm racist or anything. And I am grateful she's giving up her time to help me improve my game.

So I try.

'Th-th-thanks f-for –'

I know exactly what she's thinking. 'Stammer' and 'stupid' mean the same thing to most people.

I wait for her to laugh at me but her expression doesn't change.

'Th-thanks f-f—,' I mumble.

'Go on.'

'Th-thanks f-for c-coaching me,' I croak finally.

'You are most welcome,' she says, and spins the board round on its turntable. 'Better get started.' Maryam reaches for a laptop on the chair next to her. 'First thing I will show you is a way of getting much better at Scrabble without even touching the board. Intriguing, yes?'

She gives me a quick demonstration of some word-game software.

'It is a word-study tool, used by the top players. You must schedule in half an hour each day to train on it,' Maryam says, closing the laptop again. 'Within one week or perhaps two, you will notice improvement in your play.'

I like the idea of training up on software, and for the first time, I feel relieved that Dad is away in Brighton. He moans about the amount of time I'm spending on the computer as it is.

Maryam glances at her watch.

'We have time for a quick game. Let's see what you can do, Finlay McIntosh.'

I put my tile bag on to the table.

'Pretty,' she says, running a finger over the delicate embroidery. 'Did you sew this?'

She gives me a cheeky grin.

'M-my m-mum.' I scratch at a mark on the tabletop.

Mum would've loved the fact I was training with Maryam, an ex-national player.

'Does she play Scrabble with you, your mother? What is her name?'

I shake my head and look down at my hands. I don't know why I'm letting it get to me.

'I am so sorry,' Maryam says, softly. 'Have I upset you?'

I shake my head. 'Her n-name is Ch-Christa. Sh-she l-left.'

Maryam looks at me for a long moment but she doesn't say anything else about Mum.

We select our first seven tiles and I draw first turn.

'Let's go.' Maryam starts the timer.

I shuffle my letters around and will my fingers to stop wobbling. Nothing jumps out at me from my rack. I can't get the letters to start joining up in my mind.

I can almost feel Maryam's eyes burning into the top of my head as I slump over my tiles.

Twenty seconds before the end of my turn, I come up with pathetic L-A-C-E. Twelve measly points.

I don't want to look at Maryam, but after a few seconds I glance up anyway. She isn't laughing, she isn't looking at me at all. She is focused on her tile rack like it's the only thing in the room.

She plays J-E-T-E-S for fourteen points.

Then she spins her tile rack around to show me her letters. It feels like I'm cheating.

'Don't look so shocked,' she laughs. 'This is how you will learn.'

She points to her rack.

'Do you see how I could have played J-E-L-L-Y for twenty points using the double-letter square and the L of your word?'

She's going easy on me. She played a word worth fewer points because she thinks I'm useless.

'I am playing *tactically*,' Maryam explains. 'Now I have used up the available E and the triple-letter square, I am guessing you will find it far more difficult to get a decent score from the other letters.'

Let me get this right. She's choosing the best word to put obstacles in my way, making my game more difficult. She's not being kind, she's being *ruthless*.

'If I can force you to miss a couple of turns because I am using all the best letters, your overall score is going to suffer, see?' She smiles like she's doing me a favour.

I do see, and I can't help smiling too. It's a different approach I've never considered before.

Maryam glances at my tile bag and then her eyes lock on to mine. 'In Scrabble, as in life, the most obvious action is not always the most effective.'

PLAYERS CAN ONLY PLAY
ONE WORD PER TURN.

Second period in the afternoon is Biology and we are learning about animal behaviour.

I ignore the tight, wet balls of chewed-up paper that Oliver and his gang ping over at me. Every so often, one hits my back or my head and his gang all make a dinging noise. I ignore that, too.

'Can't you move somewhere else?' one of the girls on my row hisses at me.

I look around but there's only one spare seat right at the back on Oliver's row.

We've got a supply teacher this session because our usual teacher is off ill. The stand-in teacher has come up with a quiz. She numbers the class rows, one to five. 'So to recap, all rows will compete against each other. Each row is presented with a question and if that row gets it wrong, or doesn't know the answer, it's up for grabs for extra points to the other rows.'

The questions start easy and get harder. Ten minutes

in, all the rows are on level pegging and the teacher ups the difficulty.

'Row one, what is the term used for the process where ducklings and other baby birds recognize their mother immediately after hatching?'

Row one look blankly at each other.

'Dunno, miss,' someone mutters.

'Anyone else?' She scans the class.

I happen to know that the process is called *imprinting*, discovered by Konrad Lorenz, an Austrian scientist. But if I volunteer and try to say the word 'imprinting', I know I'll be lucky to get past 'imp'. So I don't raise my hand.

Nobody speaks up.

'OK, so that process is called *imprinting*,' the teacher confirms. 'Write it down in your exercise books, please.'

Row two get their question wrong: an example of instinctive behaviour in animals.

I can think of two examples; a spider building a web or a newly hatched turtle moving towards the sea. I stay quiet and nobody else answers it.

'Row three,' the teacher calls. 'Bats, owls and hamsters are active during the twilight hours. What do we call animals who display this type of activity?'

'Nocturnal, miss,' someone on row three calls out.

'Good try but that's the wrong answer, I'm afraid. Anyone else?' the teacher looks around the class.

The answer is *crepuscular*, like Neville.

Heat channels through my face and hands. The bottom of my back is hot and damp.

If I can call the answer out, my row will move ahead, we might even win the quiz.

I repeat the word silently. *Crepuscular.*

It sounds fine in my head, with no stammer mucking it up. I really want everyone to see that I know the answer. For once, I want to be the smart one in class, like I used to be before the stammer got worse.

My fingers are wriggling, my arm is itching to fly up into the air.

The teacher's eyes fix on to mine. She recognizes the signs that I might speak up.

'Your name?' she consults her class plan.

'F-F-Fi—'

She opens her eyes wide, questioning again. 'Name?'

I imagine the back row, just waiting for me to mess it up. I take a deep breath and try again.

'F-F-Fi—' It just won't come.

Oliver and friends erupt into hysterical laughter but the teacher has finally clicked that I'm finding it difficult.

'Come on, you can do it. Take your time, we're all behind you.'

'Yeah, we're behind him all right and it's not a pr-pretty si-sight,' Oliver quips.

The other rows turn round to watch me.

It feels like someone's holding a Bunsen burner close

to my face. I think my whole head might actually blow off any second.

'Miss, he's useless, he can't even –'

'One more word out of you and the whole class gets a detention.' She points her finger at Oliver and everyone groans. 'We'll be respectful and wait until this young man can tell me his name.'

She raises her eyebrows and smiles at me. 'Your name?'

'J-J-Jack,' I manage.

I can say Jack. I can't say Finlay without a real struggle. Some days, I can't say Finlay at all.

'Miss, he's an idiot, his name isn't –'

'Enough,' the teacher snaps, glaring Darren into silence. 'Now, *Jack*, are you going to have a go at answering the question?'

Muffled laughter from the back row.

I take a breath. Can I risk it?

If I break it into two halves, the word might be easier to say. I can do it.

Crep-uscular.

If I put my mind to it, I know I can do it.

'It's n-no use asking J-Jack, m-miss,' Oliver yells from the back. 'W-we'll be here all d-d-day.'

Pockets of sniggering break out around the class.

'Do you know the answer or not, Jack?' the supply teacher asks, impatient now.

My fingers stop wriggling.

I shake my head.

The word is still there, wanting to be spoken, but I swallow it down like a lump of cold gristle.

'Well, that *was* a hard one,' she sighs. 'The answer is *crepuscular*. Write it down, please.'

AFTER EACH TURN, PLAYERS SELECT
FURTHER TILES FROM THE TILE BAG.

Soon as the bell rings, I grab my bag and head for the classroom door. Dad's in Brighton so no lift tonight but if I can get a head start and get on the bus first, I might avoid running into Oliver.

I can see the first school bus is in and it's filling up fast.

'How you doing, J-Jack?' Oliver clamps his hand down hard on my shoulder and his mates gather round us. 'It is J-Jack, isn't it?'

I try to shrug his hand off but he grips harder, even though he's using his bad arm which is still in a sling. Other students stream out of the school on either side of us but nobody gives us a second glance, they all just want to get home.

'My shoulder's almost back to normal now, so I thought I might repay the compliment,' Oliver snarls. 'I could've reported you but I kept my mouth shut, so I could give you this.'

He reaches for something Mitchell is holding and I see too late, it's a cricket bat.

I manage to get my hand up just before Oliver cracks the bat down but my elbow takes a hit. I cry out in pain.

'That's the first time I've heard him say owt without stuttering,' Darren says.

Oliver laughs. 'It's his fingers I want. Let's see him play Scrabble when a couple are broken. Hold him still, lads.'

'St-stop!' I yell. 'St-stop it!'

Darren and Mitchell grab an arm each and Oliver moves in front of me, pulling his arm out of his fake sling so he can get a better swing with the bat.

His face is pale and dotted with angry, red spots. His eyes look crazed and dark.

I feel like I can't get enough air. I think I'm going to be sick.

'Hold his hand in front, Daz,' Oliver instructs. He begins to raise the bat.

'Move on, lads, you're causing an obstruction,' Mr Homer calls from the entrance steps. I twist round to catch his attention and he frowns, takes a few steps forward. 'What's happening here?'

'Nothing, sir, just having a bit of fun,' Oliver calls and drops the bat down by his side, out of Mr Homer's sight.

Darren and Mitchell release my arms and the three of them push through the crowd towards the bus.

Oliver turns back and grabs my arm.

'I'll get you next time and there's nothing you can do about it. You'll never get the better of me, you wimp.'

I shake him off and start to move in the opposite direction. As I walk, I pray my legs won't buckle and give way.

It takes me about forty minutes to walk home from school. It feels strange when I open the front door and step into the house. The silence feels thick and heavy, like it doesn't want me there.

I close the door behind me, leaving my bag and shoes in the hallway.

My elbow throbs where Oliver whacked it. When I touch it, I can tell there's going to be a big bruise soon.

In the sitting room I sit by the window but I don't put the telly on.

A group of teenagers I recognize from my year at school walk by, rollerblades slung over their shoulders. The boys wear beanie hats and the girls have their hair tied up in ponytails. Roller Planet is on the Castle Marina retail park, about a twenty-minute walk from here, but I've never been. I've heard people at school saying there's dance music and flashing lights. I imagine it's a bit like the ten-pin bowling place me and my mates used to go to in Mansfield.

When you sit quietly, the house isn't as silent as you

first think. Our ancient refrigerator buzzes for one thing. A dog barks nearby and I can hear kids playing football in the next street, squealing and laughing.

We had a different house and different neighbours before Mum left. You could sometimes hear three-year-old Jack who lived next door, clonking the wall with his toys as he walked upstairs. His brother, Seth, was my class. A group of us used to play cricket up the top end of our street, away from where the cars were parked.

Later, when we went in, Seth used to play his electronic keyboard but Mum and Dad never minded the noise coming through the wall. I'd probably still be mates with Seth now if we hadn't moved. I'd probably have loads of friends.

Dad said it was best we made a fresh start in a new place once Mum left, but it didn't really feel like that. It felt like we were running away.

He kept saying it would get easier. He said that given time, we'd make a great, new life for ourselves, just me and him. He'd smile when he said it but his eyes still looked just as sad.

I remember asking him how long it would take, but he didn't have an answer.

There's a theory that it takes ten thousand hours of practice to get really good at something.

'Bill Gates got access to a high school computer at the age of thirteen. That's how he got his ten thousand hours of programming in,' Mum said.

'And in the ten thousandth hour he created Microsoft!' Dad grinned. 'So what are you waiting for, Finlay?'

Mum always used to laugh at the sarky stuff Dad said, but the last few months before she left, his joking around just seemed to make her angry.

'You can achieve anything you want to, Finlay,' she'd say, looking straight at me and ignoring Dad. 'So long as you put in the hours and believe in yourself. Never let anyone tell you that you can't do it. Especially people with zero ambition.'

Dad didn't laugh then.

The ten-thousand-hour theory doesn't apply to everything. I reckon I've spent a hundred thousand hours trying to figure out why Mum left and I'm still no nearer to the truth. But I guess the theory might just come in useful for getting me to the Scrabble championships.

If I can put the hours in and forget about the fact that I'll have to talk in public, I might have a chance of pulling it off.

I've got plenty of time to think of an excuse if I change my mind. I could say I've got laryngitis or something. If I convinced Mrs Adams and Maryam I was ill, that would definitely get me out of it.

Worries are buzzing around my brain like wasps in a glass of pop. They crowd in, angrily, demanding answers. I can't seem to find out what I need to know about Alex's mum during our online chats. Deep down, I know the idea that his stepmum and my mum are the same person can't possibly be true. But I can't let it go. Not until I know for sure.

I've also been thinking about how cool it would be to meet up with Alex if he came to Nottingham. I know that can't happen unless I start to trust him, tell him where I live and stop worrying about him finding out about my stammer. It's great chatting online like normal mates. So surely there's no harm in telling him a bit more about me.

'How do you know this person isn't a pervert?' Maryam had asked me, when I told her I'd really like to meet up with Alex.

'I j-just know,' I said.

'So, now you have developed psychic abilities that allow you to see who you are playing online? This will be very useful in your gameplay, Finlay.'

I wished I hadn't bothered mentioning it to her at all. 'I c-can just t-tell, OK?'

Maryam looked thoughtful. 'There *is* one way you can be sure,' she'd said eventually. 'Skype him.'

I hadn't thought about doing that.

*

The 5.32 to Lincoln rumbles past the back of the house and I realize I've been sitting staring out of the window for nearly an hour.

My stomach is grumbling, so I head into the kitchen to make a sandwich. Dad's left some bread and when I look in the fridge I see there's a slab of cheese and a pack of fat sausages.

Later, Alex and I start a game online.

Fancy a chat on Skype? I type in the message box.

Sure! His reply comes straight back. **Give me five mins. You start.**

So much for Maryam's suspicious mind.

I play my first move and check Skype is open and that my webcam is on. After seven minutes, I check back to see if Alex is ready for our call.

You all set up? I ask. **What's your Skype name? I can call you now.**

My digital clock ticks on a couple more minutes. I look out of the window at the endless grey sky, scudded over with clouds.

Maybe my message didn't send properly. **You set up now?** I try again. **Shall I call you?**

The screen flickers and I look at the online Scrabble board. It doesn't look quite right and then I realize why.

There is no little head and shoulders icon on his side. Alex is no longer online.

*

It's nine o'clock and I don't feel tired at all. I sit down next to Neville's cage and wait for him to get up.

After a few seconds, I hear shuffling inside his house.

'Hello, Neville,' I call softly, laying down on my front and pressing my face up to the bars. His little furry face appears in the doorway of his plastic house. He sniffs the air and walks over to me.

'Crepuscular, crepuscular, crepuscular,' I say.

Neville snuffles and moves away to inspect his food bowl.

'Maryam is s-suspicious of Alex,' I tell him. 'If we'd Skyped, I could've proved he's who he says h-he is. But now . . .'

Neville has found the bits of broccoli I'd sprinkled in his food bowl earlier.

'Maybe something came up at home and A-Alex had to log off suddenly,' I say. 'I mean, stuff h-happens, right? Maybe his stepmum has found out he's chatting online to a boy c-called Finlay.'

As I say the words, my eyes prickle. Only an idiot would fantasize that such a far-fetched thing could happen.

But I can't stop doing it, I just can't.

'Maybe Alex is t-telling her all about me, *right now*.'

Neville looks up sharply from his food. His cheeks have expanded like tiny puffballs, full of broccoli and seeds. His beady black eyes bore into me. Even Neville can't stretch the truth this far.

He turns and scurries back into his little house, as if he can't wait to get away from my ridiculous ideas.

PLAYERS MUST KEEP THEIR LETTER RACKS REPLENISHED WITH A TOTAL OF SEVEN TILES THROUGHOUT THE GAME.

Saturday

My first thought when I wake up on Saturday morning is that there's no school today, no Oliver to dodge.

My second thought is that it's Dad's second night away in Brighton.

I lie in bed, staring up at the ceiling.

My elbow is sore and bruised, and the silence of the house fills my head until it's almost like a roar.

I run through all the things I could do while Dad's away, all the infinite possibilities.

I could actively *not* eat chips or beans or sausages or flaming fish fingers, for a start.

I could go bowling or to the cinema and hang around the market square afterwards. I could lean against one of the massive stone lions outside the Council House and watch the goths and the drunks squaring up to each other.

I could get the last bus home and walk through

Victoria Park, where several people have been mugged recently, just to feel the fear and survive it.

OK, maybe not that last one.

The point is, I could do all these things and more, if I wanted to. But it is all stuff that's not a lot of fun to do on your own.

Maybe Alex and I could hang out sometimes on the weekends, after we've finally met up. I'm sure Dad would be fine if Alex wanted to stay over at ours, he's desperate for me to have some mates.

I spend the morning in bed, watching old *Star Wars* DVDs. Darth Vader is my favourite character because James Earl Jones, who plays him, used to have such a bad stammer when he was a kid, he stopped talking altogether. He mostly just breathes heavily in *Star Wars* but he's also the voice of Mufasa in *The Lion King*, which proves he finally got rid of his stutter. It can be done.

Every few minutes I check on my computer to see if Alex has logged in yet but his player icon is greyed out each time.

When I eventually get dressed and go downstairs, the silence is waiting for me. I stop thinking about stuff I can do while Dad's away and focus on the one thing making me feel twitchy.

Why haven't I heard anything from Alex?

*

To distract myself, I go up to Green's Windmill. George Green was fourteen in 1807, when his dad built the windmill, and George used to work in it. He grew up to be a self-taught mathematical physicist and we learned at school that Green's Theorem and Green's Function are still used by scientists and engineers all over the world today.

The windmill is always busy on a weekend so I don't bother going inside. I've seen it all loads of times and my favourite bit is the stone floor.

The sails need to turn in the wind to get the great spur wheel turning. All the other mechanisms have to engage to grind the grain into flour, which then drops down a chute into sacks on the floor below. Lots of things have to happen in sequence before the miller gets a bag of flour.

I'll have to do lots of investigating to find out all the facts before I finally find my mum. If I get everything sorted and in the right order, it could happen. Even if the evidence seems a bit far-fetched.

I move to the far side of the windmill and look up. The big sails dwarf me but when I lean against the rough brickwork, I feel safe, like I belong here. I wonder if that's how George Green felt. He'd have definitely walked all around here, exactly where I'm standing now, sorting stuff out for his dad.

Lugging bags of flour up and down all day when you'd rather be writing mathematical formulae sounds like a tough job. If it was 1807 now, I'd probably be friends with George, although it wouldn't be much fun hanging around with someone who just wanted to do maths all day.

It's nearly dark when I get back home and I'm hungry, so I make some toast, pour a glass of juice and take them back up to my room.

I force myself to wait ten minutes before turning on the computer. I make up this silly rule that says every minute I wait will increase the chance of Alex being there by five per cent. Maybe it's not just nonsense because when I do log in, there is a green dot next to Alex's ID icon.

What happened last night? I fire off right away.

Soz, computer crashed, he sends back.

But now it's OK? He seems to be using his computer now, no problem.

Yep, stepmum is a computer whizz, even better than I am. Thought it was busted but she's sorted it. And then: **Webcam knackered so can't Skype.**

My heart tries to leap up into my mouth. *My* mum is an IT expert – brilliant at solving any computer problems we had in the house. Here's my chance to ask him straight.

What's her name?

There's no response. Radio silence from Alex.

I watch his ID icon, expecting it to blink off any

second. But it doesn't. He stays online.

Parents have banned me from talking about family stuff online, Alex messages back. **They're REALLY private. Secretive, even. Like they're trying to hide something.**

Private. Secretive.

That doesn't make sense, unless . . . unless Mum's trying hard not to be found.

If it *is* Mum. I might be totally blowing this stuff up in my mind, but it feels like the stakes just got raised.

Sucks, I know, he says. **But you're secretive about your mum too. Maybe . . . no, it doesn't matter.**

Maybe what? I ask.

Maybe we can share a secret each. It will help us to trust each other.

I haven't got any secrets, I say.

Everyone has secrets. He adds a little winking face icon to his message. **Even things you might suppose nobody else is interested in.**

When are you coming to Nottingham? I type quickly. **That's my secret! You asked where I lived and the answer is Nottingham.**

Not a very exciting secret! Dunno, Dad keeps changing his work plans, Alex sends back.

It's not the answer I was hoping for. He doesn't even seem that interested.

Dad's working in Manchester next week. Might

be Nottingham the week after that, he types.

My heart sinks.

At first I was hoping to meet up with Alex just to hang out for a day as proper mates. But now I know his dad and stepmum might be trying to hide something, the idea that his stepmum could be Mum doesn't feel as crazy any more.

My brain feels like it's overheating.

Defo meet up tho, when I do come that way, Alex types. There's a grinning icon next to his words.

I let out a long breath. I'm trying really hard not to scare Alex away by telling him my suspicions about his stepmum. He might write me off as a weirdo.

You got a coffee shop near to where you live? he asks.

Yep. One just down the road.

Cool, we can meet up there, he says. **What branch is it?**

It isn't a chain coffee shop, so it hasn't got a branch name.

It's called Coffee 'n' Cream, just at the bottom of Mundella Road. Anyone can tell you where that is, I say.

Is that just round the corner from you?

Yeah, my house is just at the top of the hill, I tell him.

I want Alex to visit. I'm certain he is who he says he

is, despite Maryam's suspicious mind. But I wonder what his face will look like when he realizes his new friend can't string a sentence together.

OK, will defo let you know which day I'll be coming, Alex says. **Be thinking about a real secret to share, one worth knowing. Have to go now.**

I sink into my chair, my mind whirling. The house is still and silent. I don't know why it feels so different when Dad's away. He's always out working anyway.

When Alex knows which day he's visiting, I'll suggest we both bring photos of our families. Then I'll know for sure about Mum without sounding like a crazy person. Or is it crazy enough to ask to see a photo of someone's family?

I hear a noise downstairs, a sort of rattling. It sounds like it's at the back of the house.

I look out of my bedroom window but I can't see or hear anything. I wait a couple of minutes and just keep watch.

A train approaches, rumbling and whirring in the distance, before whooshing by in a blur of blue and yellow. The passengers' faces light up for a second or two and I wonder if they can see the face of a boy at his bedroom window, looking back at them.

Then the train is gone and silence falls again.

Our patch of garden has thorny bushes all around the edge of it. Somebody could easily scramble across the railway tracks and hide in there, if they wanted to.

I'm still gazing down at the bottom of the garden when a quick movement catches my eye. I look down but whatever it was has gone.

It's probably just next door's cat . . . although the voice in my head says it moved more like a person.

I walk away from the window and on to the landing. The stairs are steep and narrow and the house is quite new so none of them creak.

I probably wouldn't be able to hear anyone creeping upstairs, especially if I was asleep.

I don't want to go to bed yet.

Saturday, 16 May
Dear Mum,

I don't know why I went into Dad's room. It's been ages since I've been in there.

Actually, that first bit's not strictly true. I've got a pretty good idea why I went in. I was looking for something. I don't know what, exactly. And I was feeling a bit creeped out by some noises I'd heard downstairs, if I'm honest.

Dad was never very good at cleaning when you were still here, Mum, but I don't think he ever throws anything away at all now. Useless stuff is folded up in piles, stacked all around the edge of the room and halfway up the walls. Old magazines and your antique doll collection. Useless bits of wood he's been given and even some of the old camping equipment that you'd put in the shed ready to throw out.

I didn't realize Dad had brought all this stuff with him. He must've kept it up in the loft for ages before bringing it down. There are even some heaps of your old clothes, all folded up and looking a bit dusty.

I don't know why he's keeping all this stuff; soon he won't be able to get in his bedroom at all. Sometimes I think Dad knows more than he lets on about why you walked out. I don't have any EVIDENCE [14], it's just a feeling I have.

You always used to tell me to trust my gut – that if I listened to my inner voice, I wouldn't go far wrong. Dad used to laugh at that. He'd tell you to stop filling my head with mumbo-jumbo.

Since I've been talking to Alex online, I can't push thoughts about you to the back of my mind any more. I used to believe Dad when he said it was for the best to forget everything about you. I used to think I had no choice.

But lately I've started feeling like there *is* a real chance of finding you. Maybe through the Scrabble championships, maybe through Alex – but the tiny spark of hope I used to bury deep in my chest feels like it's grown into a little FLICKERING [20] flame.

I was in the room for just a few seconds when my eyes settled on that small wooden chest in the corner. You used to keep your paperwork in there, remember?

I walked over to it and I peeked inside the lid, expecting to see just an empty space, but the chest wasn't empty at all. It was full, almost to the brim, of photographs.

I knelt down in front of it and I pulled out handful after handful of pictures that I never even knew existed, and I looked through every single one of them.

It was only when I got to the end that I realized my face was wet.

The photographs were all heaped up on the floor like a bonfire of happy memories that nobody but me cares about any more.

I pulled myself together and decided to put them all back. And that's when I spotted a folded-up square of newspaper jammed in the bottom left-hand corner of the chest. It took ages to wiggle it free without tearing it.

The newspaper is dated a week after you left us. And there's a scrawled phone number just under the SERRATED [9] edge at the top of the page.

At first I thought it was just a stupid travel article. But then I realized.

Bunny, Nottinghamshire.

That's the place you were born, Mum.

And it's only about fourteen miles from our house.

So this is what I'm thinking now: why would Dad go to the trouble of cutting out and keeping a newspaper report about somewhere so close to where we live? He said he'd piled all your stuff into the car and taken it down to the council tip. He told me he'd got rid of all the photographs of you, too.

It was all lies.

I copied the number down and put the newspaper back into the bottom of the chest. But when I started to pile the photographs back, it felt like I was pushing the memories of you away again, like a dark secret.

I don't know what all this means yet. All I know is that I definitely found something SIGNIFICANT [17].

It's just a feeling. But it's all I've got and I'm holding on to it.

Love,

Finlay x

IF A PLAYER SUCCEEDS IN USING THEIR FULL RACK OF TILES – SEVEN LETTERS – THIS IS CALLED A 'BINGO BONUS'.

Sunday

The next morning, I wake at 5.06 a.m.

Sunrises are worth getting up for, even if you wake up by mistake like I have.

The sky is streaked vivid orange and pink, like an artist drew it with a fine paintbrush. If I made a picture like that at school, Mrs Corner would say the colours need softening to make it more realistic. To get a good mark in Mrs Corner's class, your picture has to match what she has in *her* head, not your own.

I've hardly slept at all but the weird thing is, the second my eyes snap open and I see that sky, I feel full of energy and determination.

The sun is completely risen now and hangs in the sky like a massive overripe blood orange, setting the walls of my bedroom on fire.

My mind has worked overtime all night and I've finally decided what my next move should be. But it's far too early yet to take any action, so I decide to get up and have a shower.

As I step out of the tub and grab a fusty-smelling towel that's been there for ages, I force myself to focus on the very important task I've set out to do this morning.

Dad has said *so* many times he doesn't know where Mum is and that he wants to forget everything about her. So why save all her stuff and the photographs? Why hide an article about the village she was born, with a telephone number on it?

It looks like Dad has had a way of contacting her all this time.

While I eat breakfast, I take out the scrappy piece of paper from my jeans pocket and flatten it out on the table. Today could be the day I get to speak to Mum again.

At ten o'clock exactly, I take our cordless phone into the living room and I dial the number written down on the piece of paper.

Just as I think nobody is going to answer, I hear a voice – but in a flash, my hopes are dashed. It's an answerphone.

'Good morning, Bunny Post Office is now closed. We are open Monday to Friday nine until—'

Bunny Post Office? I don't hear the rest of the recording until the words: 'please leave a message after the tone.'

The machine beeps.

I take a breath.

'I – I –'

The silence of the answer machine is almost worse than speaking to a real person.

'C-c-could y-you pl—'

The words are bouncing against the roof of my mouth and back down my throat again, like an out of control ping-pong ball. I just want to know if Mum works there.

'D-does Chr—'

I'm cut off by a continuous tone. The answerphone has decided I have had enough time to make my point.

I walk back into the kitchen and get a glass of water. I take a few deep breaths and then I punch in the numbers again.

I go through the same palaver and wait for the beep so I can start speaking.

'C-could y-you tell m-me if Ch-Christa –'

Just say it, you idiot.

I open my mouth to try again but nothing comes out at all. Then I hear a sharp click and the continuous tone sounds, cutting me off again.

I bite my inside lip hard and a metallic taste fills my mouth. I feel like screaming but that won't get me anywhere. So I try a third time, taking a deep breath . . . but the beep never comes. Instead, a toneless, robotic voice informs me, 'Sorry, this voicemail is full. Please try again later.'

I snatch up the glass of water and throw it hard against the wall.

THE BINGO BONUS SCORE IS WORTH FIFTY POINTS, AND IS GIVEN IN ADDITION TO THE VALUE OF THE WORD PLAYED.

Monday

I found a note from Dad this morning, apologizing that he'd had to go out early on a job. Even though he was clattering around loud enough to wake the dead when he got back late last night, I was pleased he was home again and slept much better.

Double English to get through this morning . . . with Oliver . . . who finds it hilarious we're covering speaking and listening skills.

'Hear that, F-Finlay? You have to speak *c-c-clearly*,' he hisses loudly from the back.

'Quiet, please.' Miss Bell scowls. 'I want you all to think carefully about your class presentation. You can choose any subject you like.'

I copy down the presentation dates the teacher puts on the whiteboard before meeting Maryam, as arranged, in the library.

'So, how did it go?' she asks.

I look at her.

'The Skype session with the mysterious Alex?'

'It d-didn't w-work out,' I say, untying my tile bag. 'Alex's w-we—, his w-we—'

The words stick fast but Maryam waits anyway.

'His w-webc-cam –'

I slam the tile bag down and run my hand through my hair.

'Try taking in a deep breath before you speak and then just say the words really quickly in one outbreath. She takes in a big gulp of air. 'Just-say-the-words-quickly-with-no-gaps-like-this.'

It sounds like she's pushing the words out whether they want to come or not.

I look at her.

'Up to you.' She shrugs. 'Perhaps it is worth a try?'

I look around to check there is nobody sitting close to us. Mrs Adams is over in the far corner of the library, sorting through a box of newly delivered books.

I take a breath.

And I let it out again without speaking.

It's not going to work. It's easy for Maryam to demonstrate it because she hasn't got a stammer.

I stick my hand in the tile bag and line my seven letters up on the tile rack.

Maryam does the same. She doesn't look at me.

My turn first. I play E-X-A-M.

112

Maryam shakes her head.

'Bad move,' she mutters.

I wouldn't call a score of twenty-six a bad move for my first word.

I clamp my mouth shut and pick four new tiles.

'You need to save your power tiles until you can utilize them on a high-scoring square,' she says. She wiggles her fingers at the board. 'This? This is just a waste of your powerful letter X. Do you see that, Finlay?'

It's just a stupid practice game, I don't know why she's making such a big deal about it.

'Perhaps you are thinking I am causing some trouble over this,' Maryam says. 'But this is important. You must choose carefully when to use your power. This will get you results that can win.'

There's a commotion over by the doors as Oliver and his friends enter the library. Oliver's arm is no longer in a sling. He points over to us and says something behind his hand. They all laugh loudly.

Mrs Adams pushes the box of books aside and walks over to them.

'We've come to see if you've got any Shakespeare in, miss,' Oliver says, and his mates titter and nudge each other.

'I'm glad to hear you're so keen to read the works of Shakespeare, Oliver.' Mrs Adams gives him a tight smile. 'Over on the far wall you'll find a shelf full of plays and poetry. I'll be watching.'

My arms feel all itchy, like they're crawling with insects. I rub at my skin and shuffle around in my seat.

'Concentrate on the game,' Maryam hisses. 'Ignore those clowns.'

I make a real effort to immerse myself in the letters and words and soon Oliver's laughter and the antics of his friends fade away and out of my circle of attention.

Maryam and I are level pegging on score all the way through and then, *bam!* She lays down B-L-A-Z-I-N-G, using the G I just played. Her Z lands on a double-letter square and the B on a triple-word score. Eighty-seven stinking points on one word.

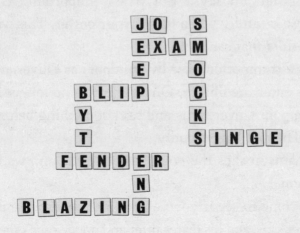

I look up at her and grin, waiting for her to crow. But Maryam isn't looking at me and she isn't grinning back.

Her face looks tight and strange like she's not sure what to do.

A LIGHT BLUE SQUARE DOUBLES THE SCORE OF THE LETTER TILE PLACED ON IT.

Maryam's attention is focused on something behind me.

Then I hear Oliver's sneering voice. 'Not bad for a girl. Especially a greasy headscarf girl, who stinks of curry.'

Maryam smells sweet, like coconut. The wisps of hair that sometimes escape her headscarf are strong and shiny.

I turn round to look for Mrs Adams but I can only see the back of her head in the storeroom, right over in the far corner of the library.

'H-hey,' I say, standing up. 'D-don't –'

'D-don't w-what, Finlay? C-come on, we haven't got all d-day. Say what you m-mean.'

Darren and Mitchell snigger.

'W-well?' Oliver says. 'Tell you what, just say your name, then. Anybody can do that, right? Even a three-year-old can say their own name. Just say "My name is Finlay McIntosh", and I'll leave you alone.'

'Ignore him, Finlay, they are not worth the effort.' Maryam stands up and begins putting the lettered tiles back in the bag.

'The effort to do what, Headscarf?' Oliver snaps. 'To say his name, to speak? Speaking is the most natural thing in the world, unless you're an ignorant foreigner or a st-stammerer, that is.'

'That's right,' adds Darren, pushing the board hard, so the tiles scatter across the table.

I hear the storeroom door close and glance hopefully across the room but Mrs Adams is standing just outside the library now, talking to a student.

'Can you smell something, F-Finlay? I suppose you must like that foreign stink, you spend all your time with her.'

Oliver takes a step closer and Maryam's whole body stiffens. Her usually lively brown eyes seem paler somehow and she doesn't try to defend herself against Oliver's nasty words. She just stares ahead, as if her mind has gone to another place.

'What you hiding under that headscarf, anyway? You got a bomb tucked away under there?' Oliver kicks out but Maryam steps back.

'Blimey, I thought I heard something ticking,' Darren says in a scared voice, and the three of them fall about laughing.

'England is for the English,' Oliver snarls.

I see his arm begin to rise, his hand forms a claw shape and moves towards Maryam's headscarf. I launch myself, throwing my full weight at him. He staggers sideways and falls, yelping as the corner of a table bites into his thigh muscle.

Mrs Adams steps back into the library, just as I slam into Oliver.

She strides over.

Oliver wails and sinks to the floor, clutching his leg and writhing around in an Oscar-winning performance.

'What on earth is going on here?' Mrs Adams says as she helps Oliver to his feet.

'H-he w-was –' I try to explain but my tongue feels all swollen and the words tuck themselves away under it.

'Finlay just attacked him, miss,' Mitchell blurts out. 'For no reason.'

'N-no h-he –'

'We were just minding our own business, miss,' Darren says, wide-eyed with innocence.

Mrs Adams looks at me for a response but all my sentences have broken into tiny pieces in my mouth.

'Maryam? What happened here?'

I wait for her to speak up for us both. I wait for her to tell Mrs Adams about Oliver's racist words and how aggressive he's been. But she doesn't answer.

'Maryam? Can you tell me what just happened?' Mrs Adams tries again.

Maryam shakes her head.

'Then I have no choice but to report this whole sorry incident to your Head of Year,' Mrs Adams says to me, walking away. 'Wait there, while I get a Violent Incident form.'

'Told you I'd get you back for my arm.' Oliver leans forward, his voice dropping low. 'Let's see them put you forward for the championships now, St-stutter Boy.'

Mrs Adams summons a first-aider who suggests Oliver applies a cold compress to his leg, and he limps off, smirking when he passes me.

Maryam – who always has an answer and always has something to say – is silent, as if she's somehow folded-in on herself. I want to tell her I saw that Oliver was going to pull off her headscarf and I want to ask why she didn't defend herself to Mrs Adams when she had the chance. But I can't say any of it because my head is pounding and my scalp is crawling.

I've got this urge to pace up and down, to scratch at my arms and legs. But I don't. I sit still and silent, the same as Maryam, knotting and unknotting my fingers.

Soon, Mr Homer, the Head of Year, appears. We follow him to his office and he moves chairs around so the three of us can sit in a small circle.

'Tell me what happened,' he says.

Neither of us speaks.

'I can't help you if you won't help yourselves,' he says, glancing at Mrs Adams's report. 'Finlay, it says here you attacked Oliver Haywood. Why did you do that?'

'H-he was g-gr—'

'He was what? Giggling? Grabbing?'

I tense up and the words all stick together, like a hairball under my tongue.

'H-he was g-going t-to g-gr—'

'Marion,' Mr Homer interrupts. 'Finlay's having trouble, can you tell me what happened in the library?'

'My name is Maryam,' she says in a small voice.

'What? Oh right, *Maryam*. Now what happened?'

'Nothing,' Maryam says.

I look at her but she won't meet my eyes.

'Look, I know Oliver Haywood is no angel. If he upset you in any way, now is your chance to tell me.'

'Oliver was going to pull off my headscarf,' Maryam says, finally. 'Finlay stopped him.'

'Did Oliver actually touch you?' Mr Homer pressed.

'No . . . but –'

'You can't just go around barging into people on the strength they *might* do something, Finlay.' Mr Homer frowns. 'Oliver says he tried to chat to you both about Scrabble and that you got angry because he interrupted your game. If you're prepared to apologize to Oliver, perhaps the three of you could make amends over a game of Scrabble and we can let it go, this time.'

'I don't want Oliver Haywood anywhere near me,' Maryam says.

Her voice is still quiet but her tone is defiant.

'That's really not a helpful attitude to have, Marion,' Mr Homer says. 'I know you've had problems previously at this school and reacted in an inappropriate manner. But from what I can gather, Oliver didn't actually assault you, you just *thought* he might.'

Maryam glances at me.

'For your own sake, you must learn to fit in with the other students and try not to always expect the worst of people. Remember that integration works both ways, Marion.'

Mr Homer glances at his watch.

'Right, I'm on duty now so I've got to go back outside. So . . .' He looks at us both in turn. 'I suggest the pair of you take five minutes now to think long and hard about your behaviour before you go and apologize to Oliver. I'll be checking with him tomorrow.'

In seconds he has left the room and we're left just looking at each other.

I take a big gulp of air in and I fill it with words like Maryam showed me and I blow it out again.

'I'll-never-say-sorry-to-him.'

The words tumble out in an uninterrupted stream. My mouth hangs open and I feel the colour drain from my face. I actually said the words without a hitch.

Maryam's fingers hang in mid-air, releasing the corner of the scarf she's been twisting.

'Wow,' she whispers.

IF TWO TRIPLE-WORD SQUARES ARE USED IN ONE WORD, THE TOTAL WORD VALUE SHOULD BE MULTIPLIED BY NINE TO ACHIEVE A FINAL SCORE.

After school, I go to the Broadmarsh station and get a bus out of town to Bunny village.

It takes about twenty minutes, and I spend practically every single one of them wondering if I've finally found the place that Mum has been living all this time. I always assumed Mum would live a long way from home, maybe in a different country, even. Who'd have thought she might have been living really close to us? So close, we'd never think to ever look there.

My fingers rest against the smooth, cool surface of her photograph. I'd managed to save this one from Dad's clearing-out rampage; little did I know he'd kept hundreds more.

Perhaps Mum *works* at the Post Office and that could be the reason Dad has the number written down. When I walk in, she might be there, standing behind the counter checking a passport application or something.

Using Maryam's big-breath technique, maybe I could

even speak to her without making myself look stupid.

Today could be the best day of my life.

I hop off the bus and start walking. I'm not sure where the Post Office is but the village is small, it can't be a million miles away.

I pass an old man, shuffling along with his shopping bag. Speaking to a stranger fills me with dread but I either get the words out somehow, or admit it's been a wasted journey.

I hold Mum's photograph up. 'Ex-ex-cuse m-me, I'm l-looking for this l-lady. Ha-have you s-seen her ar-around here?'

The old man gives me a long look and takes the photo with a tremoring hand. He holds it far away and then up very close, squinting at it the whole time.

'Nah,' he says, handing it back to me. 'Never seen her around here, mi duck. Sorry.'

Just because the first person I've asked hasn't seen Mum, it doesn't really prove anything. The old man points out the Post Office, which is at bottom of the road, at the back of the Co-op. There are quite a few people in the supermarket but nobody being served at the Post Office counter.

At the back of the counter are rows of shelves stacked with different-sized brown envelopes, packaging tape and felt-tip pens.

A lady stands behind the glass partition. It isn't Mum.

'I-I'm l-looking f-for s-someone,' I manage.

I slide Mum's photograph under the gap in the glass screen.

The woman looks at me and then picks up the photo and studies it.

'Are you the boy who tried to leave a message yesterday?' she asks.

I nod. She slides the photograph back to me and shakes her head.

'Sorry, I haven't seen this person.'

I move quickly out of the shop, I need to get some fresh air. I walk up and down the main road in the village, calling at the pub, all the shops, and I even stop and ask a caretaker who is sweeping the schoolyard.

Nobody has seen Mum. I don't think she's here.

I sit on a bench on a small patch of grass near the bus stop and squeeze my eyes shut. I'm searching for a good thought, a little piece of hope, but I can't seem to find anything.

It feels like I'm in a big hall like the one at the Council House that has a really high, domed ceiling. When you shout, your voice echoes everywhere and fills the room, but within seconds it is gone.

It feels like you just imagined it and it never really existed at all.

Monday, 18 May
Dear Mum,

It's funny, but it's the little details that I hardly took any notice of when you were here that are the ones I miss the most. Like you singing to the radio and the way you'd set the table for breakfast each morning.

My drawers were always full of clean socks and undies and an ironed school shirt would be hanging in my wardrobe each morning. These are the things I really miss.

Not because they're things I have to do for myself now but because they were the things that *you* did for me that showed you were still around, even if you'd gone out for the day or had to stay overnight somewhere with work. The house was still full of you.

When we moved to this new house, I really missed my friends back home. And I missed you. If I concentrated really hard, I could just about remember the smell of your PERFUME [14], and hear you say, *'Sometimes, Finlay, you're better off acting happy even if you don't feel it inside. You can get through the day, that way.'*

I wonder now, if the times you danced around the kitchen, you were just *acting happy*. And when you squealed with delight when I came up with a seven-letter word, were you just *getting through*?

There are days when I can't remember your smell or your voice, no matter how hard I try.

Those are the days when it feels like you were never here at all.

Love,

Finlay x

A DARK BLUE SQUARE TRIPLES THE VALUE OF THE LETTER TILE PLACED ON IT.

After I've hidden my journal, I remember to delete the answerphone message from Mr Homer, informing Dad about the 'incident' with Oliver. I don't want him refusing to go to Brighton again because he thinks I've got into trouble at school.

Meeting up with Alex feels even more important after what happened in Bunny. I'd been so sure that the phone number from the newspaper cutting was going to lead me to Mum. This is not the way it was supposed to turn out.

When I log on to the game site upstairs, Alex is waiting.

Hey, he sends over. **How's your day been?**

Pretty rubbish, I send back.

Why, what's up?

If I'm going to be mates with Alex, I have to trust him. Alex could be the first good friend I've had since I left my old school. Apart from Maryam, of course.

Wanna talk about it? he sends again.

Just trouble from some creep at school, I say, playing it down a bit.

What's his name . . . so I know to avoid him when I come to Nottingham?

Oliver Haywood, I say. **Hope you never have to meet him.**

Sometimes, people like that need teaching a lesson.

Yeah, I type, grinning. **You up for a game?**

Can't. Tea ready in 15. Can chat for a bit though.

Cool.

So, have you got a decent secret to share then?

Alex's words flicker slightly in the message box, waiting for my reply. I feel like there's a kind of pressure behind them. But I have to say *something*.

OK, here's a secret – I hate ice cream!! Hardly anyone knows that about me :-D

Nothing back for a few minutes.

Then Alex's reply arrives.

I mean a REAL secret, Finlay. One you care about – one that you haven't told anyone else.

My clammy hands fall away from the keyboard.

I know I should log off, that's what you're supposed to do if you feel uncomfortable online. But I don't want to offend Alex, there's too much at stake.

In the absence of knowing what to say, I go downstairs to get a mug of tea and a biscuit. When I get back, there's another message blinking at me from the middle of the screen.

OK, my turn first. Three years ago I found out my dad was having a fling with the woman he worked with. And I didn't tell my mum.

Now I'm really lost for words. What do you say to something like that?

My mum died a year later, he goes on. **Made me feel like a proper traitor, you know?**

You shouldn't feel bad, it wasn't your fault, I type.

Nothing for a minute or two and then he replies.

I've never told anyone that before, Finlay.

My tingly fingers hover above the keyboard. Alex must trust me completely to share something that personal.

I haven't got many mates. Spend most of my time in the house since Mum died, he continues. **Embarrassing, right?**

I know how *that* feels. It's amazing how much I have in common with Alex. Mum didn't *die*, but since she went away, having mates is just a distant memory.

It's OK if you don't want to share anything with me, I understand, he says.

He must REALLY trust me to open up like he has and not expect anything back. My breathing has got faster, shallower. My hands feel a bit shaky but my fingers start

128

to type. When I've finished, I send the message before I can change my mind.

Here's my secret, the one I'm not supposed to talk to anyone about. My mum left home two years ago, just disappeared. She never said goodbye and I still don't know why she left.

I wait for Alex's shocked response but he stays quiet.

I take a gulp of tea but it doesn't help my dry mouth. Telling Alex my secret might make it easier to ask him about his stepmum. In a few minutes, if I ask the right questions, it might just be possible I have found my mum.

THERE ARE FOUR DOUBLE-WORD SQUARES ON THE BOARD.

Have you ever sat waiting for something for exactly seventy-two seconds?

I mean just sat, staring into space. Not looking at your phone or reading, or listening to music. Just waiting.

Trust me, seventy-two seconds can seem like an hour.

Just as I convince myself I've offended Alex in some way, a message flashes up.

Who says you're not supposed to talk about it? Alex asks.

I feel a tiny prick of disappointment that he isn't as shocked as I was by *his* secret. Maybe he doesn't believe me, or thinks I'm copying him, from when he first said his stepmum had left her family.

My Dad won't discuss it, I reply.

Why?

Dunno, he just doesn't like to. He got rid of all her stuff.

Everything??

Yep, everything. Well, he said he did. But I just found out he lied.

What do you mean?

I want to get off the subject of Mum's stuff and find out once and for all if my crazy theory is correct: is Alex's stepmum actually MY mum? If the answer is no, then at least I can forget all about it and concentrate on just being mates.

I take a big breath before I begin to type. **When we first started talking, you said your stepmum walked out on her family.**

That's true, Alex says. **First, tell me what you mean about your dad lying about getting rid of your mum's stuff. It's obviously bothering you.**

Alex is hanging on like a terrier. I'm going to have to tell him.

While Dad was working, I went into his room and looked around. He had lots of photographs of Mum and loads of other stuff, too.

Other stuff, like what?

How far do I go? Do I tell Alex about the newspaper cutting with the telephone number on it?

Finlay?

My fingers hover over the keys.

What else did you find?

Nothing, I type. **Just clothes and stuff he said he'd taken to the council tip.**

Alex stays silent.

I feel bad because good mates don't keep stuff from each other. Once we've met up in real life, it'll be different. I'll be able to tell him everything then. Right now, though, I can't wait any longer.

This sounds nuts, I type. **But what's your stepmum's name and where did she live before she met your dad?**

It seems ages before I get Alex's reply. The only reason I know he's still online is that his ID icon is still green.

Just as I begin to lose hope, he sends me my answer.

Her name is Nicole and I don't know where she lived before.

I feel my heart sink down inside me like a wet, cold stone.

Then the message box flashes again.

But that's not her real name. Dad told me she'd created a new identity because she did something REALLY bad.

I think I've forgotten how to breathe. I read Alex's message again.

Have you got a pic? I manage to type.

But before I can press the send button, another message from Alex pings through.

Gotta go. Speak tomoz. And he's gone.

*

After pacing around the house until nearly midnight, I somehow managed to drop off into a troubled sleep. I dipped in and out of strange places in my head. Places where I had to climb a steep, slippery incline and a giant wave of water swept over the house as I looked out of my bedroom window.

At some point I wake up to hear Neville scratching and scrabbling around in his hamster house, rebuilding his nest with bedding fluff. I wish I could curl up into a tiny ball and roll right in there with him, somewhere dark and safe where nothing bad can happen.

I can just about see his cage in the glow of the street lights.

'It's Mum, Nev, I know it,' I whisper over to him.

Neville's twitchy snout appears and he shoots me a look.

'OK, I don't know for d-definite, but it *might* be her. It really might be.'

Neville isn't impressed. He gives a snuffle and disappears back into his fluffy bed.

We break up from school this Friday and the championships are in the middle of half-term. Mrs Adams has arranged for me and Maryam to practise at the youth club while school is closed.

But the championships don't seem so important right now. All I can think about is the conversation I had with Alex. I was so stupid. I should just have told him that I think 'Nicole' could be my mum. But I couldn't bring myself to do it, in the end.

If I'm wrong then I can wave goodbye to having any mates at all. Alex will think I'm such a loser. I mean, who wouldn't?

But if I'm right . . .

My brain whirls at the thought of it.

Even though the odds are tiny, I can't let it go. I need solid proof, and that can only be gained by meeting up with Alex in person.

It's only then that I'll know for sure.

TRIPLE-WORD-SCORE SQUARES ARE FOUND ON ALL FOUR SIDES OF THE BOARD AND ARE OF EQUAL DISTANCE FROM EACH CORNER.

Tuesday

Next day I have a good morning, mainly because Oliver is in different lessons to me. When the lunch bell sounds, I go to the library to get in a quick training session with Maryam, even though my heart isn't really in it at all.

I keep my head down and look as though I'm watching and listening, but when we finish, I can't remember a single thing I'm supposed to have learned.

I can't stop thinking about meeting up with Alex. Even though I want to stay friends with him, getting the information about Mum feels more important.

'Your mind is somewhere else,' Maryam observes.

I shrug, then suddenly remember something I wanted to ask her.

'What d-did Mr Homer m-mean, yester-yesterday, when h-he said –' I take a deep breath and push the words out fast – 'you'd-acted-inappropriately-before?'

Maryam shakes her head. 'It is stuff I would rather forget about.'

I remember there was some kind of incident with sixth-form students last year, but I can't remember the details. I don't push her, it's obvious she doesn't want to talk about it.

As soon as we've finished, Maryam rushes off to see her Science tutor.

I step outside the library door and Oliver barges past with Darren and Mitchell. 'Watch out, lads, F-Finlay'll floor you if you so much as look at his stinky girlfriend.'

'L-leave her a-al-al—'

'Alone, you mean, you total jerk?' Oliver whips round. 'I don't know why you're sticking up for her, you're just her lab-rat, F-F-Finlay.'

My mouth might as well be sealed up completely but Oliver takes one look at my face and lets out a short burst of laughter.

'You don't think she's helping you with Scrabble training cos she actually *likes* you, do you?'

'Aww, he's all upset now, look!' Darren grins. 'Did you think Headscarf fancied you or summat?'

'Do you know what her latest science project's about?' Oliver demands.

'*You're* her experiment,' Mitchell yells, and punches the air.

'Wh-wh-what?' I choke.

'She was in the Science department this morning, talking to Mr Pritchard about her project on st-st-stuttering.' Oliver grins at the others. 'Turns out her p-project p-piece is studying some daft prat that can't string two w-w-words together. Oh, s-sorry, F-F-Finlay, I forgot you were here for a second.'

Before Oliver walks away, he presses hard on the top of my head with the flat of his hand. Not a slap, it doesn't hurt, it just feels like he's trying to press me into the ground and out of his way.

'G-get off m-me!'

'St-steady on, F-Finlay, d-don't have a f-fart at-attack!' Oliver pushes me aside and they walk away, laughing together.

Fifteen minutes before the afternoon bell, I find Maryam sitting on a bench in the school's nature garden, reading a book. She glances up when I sit down but then goes back to her reading.

'You have chewing gum in your hair,' she says, without looking up.

I pat around my head and feel a flat, chewed-up lump on top. I try to pull it out but it's soft and just pulls into a long string.

'You'll have to let it dry and then cut it out,' Maryam says.

'Th-that idiot, Ol-Oliver,' I curse, recalling how he

pressed his hand on my head. 'He s-said s-something. Ab-about you.'

Maryam glances round, her expression growing dark.

'He s-said you're doing a pr-pr-project.'

'Why would you believe *anything* Oliver says?' Maryam sighs.

'A pr-project ab-about m-me.'

Maryam gulps and closes her book.

'I'm not doing a project about *you* specifically, Finlay.'

'Th-that's why y-you're hel-helping me.' My face burns, I feel like I might burst into tears.

'That's not true.'

It was better when I had no friends at all. I think about Neville, all alone in his cage. He has no hamster friends who can disappoint him; he's lucky that there's nobody that can hurt him or betray his trust.

I stand up to leave.

'Finlay,' Maryam says quickly. 'Don't go, let's talk about this.'

'Ab-about wh-what? Th-that I'm an exp—' I take a breath. 'Ex-periment?'

'You are not an experiment, Finlay,' Maryam says quietly. 'I want to help you.'

'F-for your pr-project?'

'No. Not for my project.'

So there *is* a project.

'Finlay, please. I should have told you before now

138

that I want to be a speech therapist. I want to be the best speech therapist in the whole world. That has nothing to do with our friendship,' Maryam says. 'I swear.'

'Th-that's why you off-ered to h-help me with Sc-Scr—'

'No, it isn't.' Maryam's voice rises up an octave. 'And I didn't actually offer to help you with Scrabble training, Mrs Adams *asked* me to.'

THE BONUS SQUARES ARE IDENTIFIABLE BY THEIR DIFFERENT COLOURS.

I stomp off towards the Technology Block, where my next lesson is.

Me: I am the subject of Maryam's science project. Maryam grabs my arm from behind. I feel it twist and I yell and yank it away from her.

We both lose our balance and suddenly, we're in a twisted heap on the ground.

We look at each other. Maryam's mouth twitches but I look away.

I won't laugh, I won't even smile. I can't.

'Finlay, please, just stop for a moment and I will explain everything.' Maryam hauls herself up and reaches out to me.

I ignore her hand but I get up and sit on the bench. I haven't got anywhere else to go until afternoon lessons start. My body feels heavy, like I'm carrying a backpack full of rusty old weights.

'Earlier, you asked me about Mr Homer's comment,'

Maryam says. 'About some trouble I had at school, last year.'

I frown. What does that have to do with anything?

'Well, I'd just started at the school and I sort of wrecked a classroom when some kids called me names.'

Maryam wrecked a classroom? That just didn't seem possible.

Maybe I just don't know Maryam at all.

'I turned over a few tables and chairs and threw a whiteboard eraser that, unfortunately for me, smashed a small window.' She grins at my expression. 'I am a wild child, eh, Finlay?'

I don't laugh. I don't say anything.

'Of course, I regret it now. I was silly, I reacted to the idiots that were calling me names, instead of walking away and reporting them. After that, Mrs Adams offered to mentor me. She saved me from exclusion.'

The image of Maryam kicking off in the classroom is shocking, but not as shocking as the idea of kind, thoughtful Maryam being a mask for scientific, *cruel* Maryam, who just wants to study me to get top marks for her science project.

'As you are aware, I used to play in the Pakistani Scrabble youth team and with Mrs Adams being Scrabble-mad, she asked me to help out at the after-school club. When you came along, she asked me to help with your training.'

Maryam obviously likes Scrabble, so surely she would be Mrs Adams's first choice.

'W-why don't y-you enter y-yourself?'

'I like the game but I've always disliked playing competitively.' She shrugs.

I don't say anything. Thanks to Oliver, it's pretty obvious why she agreed to help with my training.

Maryam turns and places her hand gently on my shoulder.

'Finlay, I did not know about your stammer until *after* I had agreed to coach you.'

I remembered how Maryam had looked at me strangely when we played our first game. It feels like she's telling the truth.

I relax my shoulders a little but remind myself that she's still doing a project about me, an *experiment*, according to Oliver.

'My science project isn't about *you*, Finlay,' Maryam says. 'It is not even *just* about stammering, although it does cover it.'

I try and keep my face normal but I can feel it crumpling.

'Finlay, you are speaking better, more fluidly, yes?'

I don't answer her. I don't want to let her worm her way out of it all.

'It was my goal to become a speech therapist long before I met you and it is still the case now,' she says.

'My project might be able to help you with techniques that may improve your verbal control but you are not my research subject.'

Now she's talking like a scientist.

'Y-you sh-should've told me.' I press my chin into my chest.

'Yes, I should,' Maryam admits. 'I am sorry, Finlay. I never meant to deceive you, only to help you.'

Now I feel like I'm the one who has done something wrong. I don't know why I'd instantly believed Oliver over Maryam.

'People do not always have to have a hidden reason for wanting to get to know you, Finlay. You are an intelligent, interesting person,' Maryam says. 'Have you ever considered that sometimes people just like you for who you are?'

The answer is no. I've never considered that at all.

Now I know that Maryam has hit back at bullies before, the incident with Oliver in the library makes even less sense.

'Y-yesterday, you c-could've got Oliver d-done but you d-didn't say anyth-thing at all.'

'I know,' she says quietly.

'O-Oliver is an idiot,' I say. 'Nothing he s-says means anyth-thing.'

Maryam looks down at her hands.

'Yesterday it *did* mean something. To me.'

I don't say anything.

'You see, it is not the first time this has happened, Finlay,' Maryam says, turning her shining brown eyes in my direction. 'There have been many instances of people hating me, but what Oliver did yesterday, or was going to do, it took me back to a very bad place.'

I feel terrible. Maryam is such a lovely, gentle person. I can't imagine anyone hating her . . . except Oliver. But he hates nearly everything so he doesn't count.

'B-but I bet you never d-did anything b-bad to anyone in y-your life,' I say.

Maryam smiles again and I feel foolish because deep down, I know exactly the reason why people that don't even know her don't like her.

'They see this . . .' She points to her shimmering black and silver headscarf. 'And this is enough.'

BONUS SQUARES THAT OFFER ADDITIONAL POINTS CAN ONLY BE USED ONCE.

The bell for afternoon lessons sounds, but neither of us moves. I look down at the slats on the bench and rub my finger over some of the names etched into the wood; people who wanted to leave their mark, to say that they were once here.

Maryam is covered in marks from being hurt by other people, but those marks aren't visible. Today, I can feel the little pieces of her pain in the air, flapping around us like poisonous bats.

'W-why wear your headscarf, th-then?' I say. 'If it m-marks you out as being di-different, m-maybe you sh-should leave it off.'

Maryam's mouth sets and a steely look comes into her eyes.

'Never,' she says. '*They* will not decide who, or what, I am.'

'I thought y-you had to wear it,' I say. 'I m-mean like, your p-parents make you do it.'

Maryam's face softens again. 'No, it is my decision. It's a part of *my* faith, something *I* believe in,' she says. 'And some people will hate me for it.'

She's right about that.

She sits up a bit straighter and her voice turns theatrical. 'Here is an amazing fact: it is possible to wear a headscarf *and* be a confident, successful woman . . . Shock, horror!'

I laugh. Maryam's funny and I like that her eyes are dancing with mischief again.

'I wanted to tell Mrs Adams about the things Oliver said,' Maryam continues. 'I know I should have spoken up.'

She chews at a fingernail.

'When I first came to live in the UK with my family, my new school seemed such a welcoming place.'

She stares towards the playing field, her eyes glazing over.

'On my first day, my mother allowed me to wear my late grandmother's hijab. Nani had sewn on the pearls and sequins by hand for her first family outing to meet her future husband, my grandfather.'

She gives a small, sad smile and touches her own headscarf as if it gives her some comfort.

'My first day started well, but this one older boy, he took a big dislike to me before we even spoke.'

'W-why?'

'We found out afterwards that he had lost his uncle in the London terrorist bombings. It was very sad, a terrible tragedy. But he dealt with the sadness by becoming angry and aggressive towards people like me. He cornered me in the playground and began taunting me. When a big group of people gathered round I felt sure someone would help me, that someone would stop him. But nobody did.'

I think about the feeling of growing dread that takes over when Oliver and his friends surround me.

'He tore off my grandmother's headscarf and spat on it. He ground it into the dirty concrete with the heel of his shoe.' Maryam's fingers twist into the ends of her headscarf until tiny sparkling beads shower into her lap. 'He pushed me over and thumped me, kicked me.'

I reach for her hand and gently pull it away from the fabric. Her eyes are wide and staring and I know she is still back there, reliving the horror.

'It's o-over, n-now,' I say. 'N-nobody will h-hurt you here.'

'Won't they, Finlay? I'm not so sure. You stopped Oliver yesterday, but you saw what he was going to do.'

I try to think of something to say, but there is nothing.

'I thank you for doing that, Finlay. But I failed both of us when I didn't report him.' She looks down and her voice drops to a whisper. 'You see, when I spoke up at my old school and told the teachers, it just made everything worse.'

I rub my still-sore elbow and think of the times I've lied to Dad about a bruise or a torn blazer, to stop him coming into school. The teachers always think they can deal with bullies . . . but the teachers aren't always there, in the quieter corridors or the dark corner of the cloakroom. They can't stop things happening every single second of the day.

Sometimes, it might just be a push or a snigger. It might be hardly anything at all, not enough to report them for, anyway. But all those tiny things add up to something bigger that makes you hate yourself when you look in the mirror.

'I-it's not y-your f-fault,' I say gently. 'D-don't feel b-bad.'

A fat tear rolls down her face and plops on to the cover of the book in her lap.

'I thought myself stronger now, but I suppose we all try to tell ourselves that things have changed, when in fact, they've probably got even worse.'

I try to smile, but there is nothing I can say to help. Then the late bell rings, and we both get up and hurry our separate ways.

Wednesday, 20 May
Dear Mum,

Sometimes, there is the odd day that part of me feels thankful you left us.

There. I said it.

Today is one of those days. I'm glad you aren't here to see what I've turned into. I've drifted through the day like a ghost, like a person that used to exist but nobody notices any more.

When I was younger, you were always so strong. It must have SAPPED [11] your energy trying to help me with my stammer, even though it wasn't that bad then. Imagine that stammer magnified by ten times, and you'll be a bit closer to understanding what it's like now. On days like today, I feel glad you're not here because I know I'd be such a disappointment to you.

You would say, 'Speak out, Finlay. Be strong!'

But that's easier said than done.

See, nobody knows I'm different until I start to speak. That moment you see the realization dawn in their eyes – the embarrassment, the amusement, sometimes the pity – and you realize they can't wait to get away from you. That's the moment something cracks a bit inside, deep down where no one else can see.

Maryam understands because she's different too, in lots of people's eyes. Different in a way she can do nothing about. Like me.

Course, we've both found ways to try and be *less* different. I can change what I want to say at the last minute, or word-swap, to make the sentences a little bit easier to get out.

And Maryam hides away inside herself, when she should be screaming out and refusing to listen to Oliver's crap.

Nothing ever *really* works, we both know that.

Even so, I'll try anything to stop the words from falling out like broken matchsticks. Even if that means holding my tongue when I'd really like to speak.

But there's a price to be paid for trying to be invisible.

Sometimes, swallowing down words makes my throat feel raw and it makes my stomach ache. Why am I the only one at school who has to look like a JABBERING [21] idiot when I try to say my own name?

I haven't found an answer yet. I'm not sure there *is* one.

Maybe it's the same as the reason you left home, Mum. That I did something bad, that I somehow deserved it. I want you to know I'm trying hard to be better now. I'm going to make you proud of me.

I'm going to show you I'm a boy worth knowing.

Not a ghost.

Love,

Finlay x

'E' IS THE MOST VERSATILE
VOWEL TO HOLD.

Thursday

I was up until late last night, writing in my journal and thinking about how the stuff Maryam went through at her old school still affects how she feels and what she does.

I didn't get a chance to talk to her at all yesterday because the sixth-formers had their mock exams. But yesterday wasn't all bad. Oliver and his mates were on a sports trip, so I could relax for once.

This morning, it takes a couple of minutes after my alarm goes off before it dawns on me that today is the day I go head to head with Oliver. Mrs Adams will finally decide who she wants to put forward as the main contender in the school championships.

The morning goes quickly. Lessons aren't too bad; all the teachers are winding down now for their staff-training day tomorrow and I only get hit twice with Oliver's paper spit-balls.

When I get to the library at lunchtime, Oliver is already seated at the table, waiting.

'You boys get yourselves comfortable and I'll go and get two glasses of water,' Mrs Adams chirps. 'I've closed the library to general use.'

'I know that witch from Pakistan has been teaching you cheat techniques,' Oliver snarls, when Mrs Adams disappears. 'So I'll give you a choice. Let me win and I'll leave you both alone. Or there's the other choice . . . and I don't need to tell you how miserable *that* will make you and your bomber girlfriend.'

I hold Oliver's stare and a thin wire of heat rears up from my belly. If it's the last thing I do, I want to beat him in this game because I know now how much he wants to win.

'Ready to start?' Mrs Adams appears with our water.

Oliver breaks eye contact and gives Mrs Adams a sickly smile.

'Ready, miss,' he says politely. 'Your turn first, Finlay.'

It feels like there's a knot, hard as a nut, lodged in my throat.

We select our letters and Mrs Adams starts the timer.

I play C-R-W-T-H for my first word.

No vowels for him to use. No helping him in any way.

Mrs Adams taps the word into her iPad just as Oliver opens his mouth to object that it isn't allowed.

'Excellent play, Finlay.' Mrs Adams beams. 'A *crwth* is an ancient stringed instrument.'

Oliver comes back with G-R-E-W, using the W of my word.

There's a tap at the library door and I spot Maryam's face peering through the glass panel. Mrs Adams springs up to let her in.

'Careful,' Oliver whispers, plunging his hand into the tile bag. 'Make me look stupid and I will make the headscarf girl suffer.'

I reach for my letters and build up C-R-E-T-I-N underneath the C of C-R-W-T-H.

I smirk at Oliver, and Maryam gives an involuntary snort and quickly claps her hand over her mouth. Oliver's eyes flash sparks at both of us and I allow myself a small smile. Mrs Adams turns to Maryam and asks her to keep track of the scoring.

While they are speaking, Oliver leans forward.

'I don't have to lay a finger on her,' he whispers. 'I can hurt her really bad with just words.'

I think about Maryam's eyes, puddled with misery. How she stares into space when she starts thinking about what happened at her old school. The way she couldn't bring herself to tell Mrs Adams or Mr Homer exactly what Oliver had said to her.

Do I really want to put her through that and worse, just because I'm too proud to let Oliver win a silly practice game? I feel confident that Mrs Adams knows exactly who the best player is.

I ignore my high-scoring letters and play T-A-N. Three points.

Maryam is trying to catch my eye. She has full sight of my letters from where she is standing. She'll be baffled as to why I'm not playing the high-scoring words I could be.

Oliver's confidence balloons.

He plays A-X-I-S, S-T-O-R-K and J-O-B.

I play R-A-G, B-A-N and A-M.

Mrs Adams frowns.

Maryam lets out a sigh behind me.

The timer sounds and Oliver stands up, holding his fists in the air.

While I put the tiles away, he smiles widely at Mrs Adams. 'Told you I was the best, miss,' he says with a grin. Before he leaves the table, he leans forward and whispers to me. 'By the way, F-Finlay, you've still got chewing gum in your n-n-nit-infested hair.'

While Maryam speaks to a concerned-looking Mrs Adams, I race out of the library to the toilets to look in the mirror. I thought I'd managed to get all the gum out on Tuesday night, but there are still a few sticky bits clinging to my hair.

I stare at myself in the mirror. After my game with Oliver, I realize he will never leave Maryam or me alone until he's top dog at the Scrabble club again. He can't stand not being the best, even though me being chosen for the championships doesn't even affect his Duke of Edinburgh.

As I leave the toilets there is a yell.

'Finlay, wait!' Maryam flies down the corridor behind me.

I slow down but I don't stop.

'Finlay, what on earth was *that*?'

'I d-don't want to t-talk about it,' I say, striding on towards the playground and looking straight ahead.

'You're going to *have* to talk about it. Mrs Adams is actually considering withdrawing you from the championships altogether and putting Oliver forward on his own.'

The floor swims beneath me.

Maryam seems shocked by how shocked *I* look.

'Finlay, are you all right?'

I'm not all right. How could I have been such an idiot as to let Oliver get to me? Even if 'Nicole' turns out to be Mum, that's not the end of it. I need to do well in the championships to prove to her I'm a son worth having. And if 'Nicole' *isn't* Mum, then winning the championships is the only real chance I have to find her.

'Finlay!' Maryam grabs hold of my blazer collar but I shrug her off. I haven't got time to explain everything to her now – I need to get back to Mrs Adams, to convince her that I should be the one entered into the schools championships, not Oliver.

I turn back towards the library and start walking.

'Finlay,' Maryam calls. 'Please, speak to me.'

'L-leave me al-alone!' I shout, increasing my pace.

And she does. For the rest of the day.

IF A PLAYER IS NOT ABLE TO PLAY A WORD ON THEIR TURN, THEY ARE ENTITLED TO PASS, OR CAN EXCHANGE ALL THEIR LETTERS FOR NEW TILES.

I wait outside the locked library doors for the rest of lunchtime but the afternoon bell sounds before Mrs Adams returns.

As I drag myself to History, I get ready to deal with Oliver's jibes about being the one chosen to represent the school, but when I get to the lesson, Oliver isn't there. Still, I can't seem to concentrate. Soon as the final bell sounds, I grab my bag and run upstairs, hoping to catch Mrs Adams before she goes home. My luck is in; I catch her locking up.

'I've already told Oliver he's our substitute,' she says when I eventually manage to spit out enough words to make her understand that I want another chance to prove myself.

'Y-you d-did?' I haven't seen Oliver all afternoon and now I realize why. He must be furious.

'I've known you're the better player all along.' Mrs Adams nods, putting down her keys. 'But I have to be seen to be fair, and if Oliver had also taken up Maryam's offer of training and managed to improve, then I would have seriously considered him.'

I blow out a long breath.

'As I explained to Oliver, he won today not because his game had improved but because your own game slipped for some reason. If I didn't know better, I'd think you *allowed* him to win.'

I fidget but I don't reply.

'Maryam has explained to me some of the difficulties you've both had recently with Oliver,' Mrs Adams continues. 'I shall be speaking to Mr Homer about that tomorrow.'

I feel a lightness inside for the first time today – I'm so pleased that Maryam finally spoke up.

'What *I* must be sure of is that you want to enter the championships, Finlay,' Mrs Adams adds. 'I'm aware I can be a little too . . . *enthusiastic* at times.'

'Bossy' is a far better word, but I decide to keep that opinion to myself.

'I r-really do w-want to ent-ent—' I nearly manage.

'Enter? Good, well that's settled then.'

I leave the library, relieved and drained. But mostly, I feel grateful that I have another chance.

For once, the quiet calm back home feels welcoming, even though I wish Dad wasn't working away. I'm wound up inside, tight as a spring.

I find an ancient chicken tikka meal in the freezer and pop it into the microwave. I turn on the TV, scoff the ready meal and eat raspberry-ripple ice cream straight from the tub while watching three back-to-back re-runs of *Family Guy*.

I'm trying to get my mind to settle.

I wonder if I'll ever find out the identity of the mysterious 'Nicole', or make a real-life friend of Alex. The two things seem to push and pull against each other. I'm scared that only one can win.

The light is fading rapidly outside, and soon Neville will be up. I think about bringing his cage downstairs so I'll have someone to watch TV with.

Me and Neville don't need words. When his little hands grip the bars and he looks at me, I know he understands.

People who know sign language move their hands, their faces and even their bodies to communicate with others. Like Neville, they let people know how they are feeling and they don't even have to say one word out loud.

If I was deaf, people wouldn't expect me to try and speak. But I'm not deaf, so everyone just thinks I'm stupid. Why does everybody put such importance on talking out loud? The spoken word is definitely overrated.

I can't concentrate, so I turn off the TV, and that's when I hear the noise.

It sounds as if someone just rattled the handle of the back door in the kitchen.

I sit really still, as though the sound of my breath will give me away. But give me away to who? I'm not expecting a caller.

There. There it is again, a sort of rattling noise.

It's not windy out and visitors usually come to the front door and ring the bell.

My ears and hands feel hot but I'm not scared. It's nothing.

I can hear my heart thudding louder with every second.

'*Grow a pair, Finlay!*' Dad would say with a laugh, if he were here now.

I stand up and creep across the room. From here, I have a good view of the kitchen. The back door itself is solid but to the left of it is a narrow, long window, with opaque patterned glass.

I've left the key in the lock. If someone were to smash the window, they could easily put their hand through and twist the key to open the door.

It will take about six strides to get to the door and snatch the key from the lock.

I take a step forward. At that moment, a shadow flits across the glass and disappears again.

Somebody is definitely out there.

The door handle rattles again and then there is a sharp knock. My stomach drops like a dead weight and I feel the ready meal and the ice cream sloshing dangerously together.

Another rattle, another knock. Then a muffled voice.

'Finlay? It is me, Maryam. Open up.'

'One s-second,' I call.

My shoulders soften and I let out a little laugh. It sounds high-pitched and strange.

I quickly run the tap and take a deep slug of cool water, then I twist the key and open the door.

'I thought you were never going to let me inside,' Maryam says, stepping into the kitchen.

'I h-had the T-TV on,' I fib. 'You sh-should've rung the d-doorbell.'

'I remember you saying you always use the back door.' Maryam frowns and holds something out to me. 'I brought you the Advanced Anagram book I told you about last week.'

'Th-thanks,' I mumble and take the book without looking at it. I get the feeling it's not the only reason Maryam has come over.

'Finlay, I do not know what happened today. You were playing brilliantly and then you just went to pieces. You should have destroyed that idiot on the board.'

'I kn-know. A-and I'm s-sorry I sn-snapped at y-you earlier.'

'It's fine.' She shrugs her shoulders, then narrows her eyes and peers at me. 'Are you feeling OK? You look a little pale.'

'F-fancy a g-glass of juice?' I turn to the fridge.

'Sure,' Maryam says. 'But let me cut the rest of those gummy bits out of your hair first.'

After she's snipped the last of the dried-up goo out, I switch on the lamps and we sit down in the living room with our juice.

'You t-told Mrs Ad-Adams ab-about Ol-Oliver,' I say.

She nods. 'Sometimes you've just got to face things, no matter how much you are dreading it.' The wall of silence in the room has disappeared. It feels completely different in here now.

All it takes is having someone to talk to, and every-thing changes.

PASSING ON A TURN OR SWAPPING
LETTER TILES INCURS A ZERO SCORE.

While we drink our juice, I tell Maryam that despite the disastrous play-off, Mrs Adams has still chosen me to go to the Scrabble championships.

'Finlay,' she says. 'I have been meaning to ask you again about your online friend. The boy you were going to Skype?'

'A-Alex,' I nod.

'Yes, Alex. Why weren't you able to speak to him?'

'His w-webcam was b-broken.'

'I see.' Maryam's brows wrinkle together. 'Tell me, Finlay, do you and Alex chat online, or just play Scrabble?'

'We t-talk, we have lots in c-common.'

I remember how Maryam trusted me enough to share her bad experience at school. Maybe I should take a chance and do the same. Like Alex says, that's what good friends do.

'His m-mum died and he hasn't got many f-friends . . .

L-like me,' I say. 'Even th-though we haven't m-met yet, we get on r-really w-well.'

'Be careful,' Maryam says. 'You still don't know who this person is. Oh, and Finlay?'

I look at her.

'*I* am your friend.'

I smile.

I want to tell her not to worry about Alex. She doesn't understand that he's a genuine friend. She doesn't know that he might hold the key to finding Mum.

'The last time you made contact, what did you talk about?' Maryam isn't backing off.

'My m-mum,' I say, choosing my words carefully. I'm not going to betray Alex's secret about his dad's affair. 'Ab-about her leaving.'

'How did you begin such a conversation?' Maryam says.

'He j-just w-wanted to know if D-Dad got rid of all her st-stuff.'

'I do not understand why a fourteen-year-old boy would be interested in this,' Maryam persists.

I shrug.

'Tell me again what happened with your mum, Finlay,' Maryam says. 'If it does not upset you too much.'

I tell her how Mum left without saying anything or telling anyone where she was going. Maryam asks if we were close.

'Yes,' I say softly. 'Mum t-taught me how to p-play Scrabble.'

Maryam frowns and shakes her head. 'Forgive me for saying this, Finlay, but it seems astonishing that your mum would just walk out like that. Surely there is more to it.'

I try to stop my eyes tearing up by blinking really fast but it doesn't really work.

'I have upset you, I am so sorry.'

'No, it f-feels great to hear s-someone say that.' I smile. 'I n-never believed in m-my heart M-Mum w-would just l-leave.'

'In that case, you should follow your heart,' Maryam says firmly. She thinks for a moment and then smiles. 'Sometimes, in a tough game of Scrabble, it looks as if there is no chance of placing a word, but do you just give up? No, you keep looking, keep trying.' She reaches for my hand and squeezes my fingers hard. Her face grows serious. 'If you feel it in your heart, Finlay, you can be sure there is a way. You don't need Online Alex to tell you that.'

On the spur of the moment, I tell Maryam what happened today in the game with Oliver.

'He threatened you *with me?*' Her mouth twists up. 'Finlay, if you ever lose a game again because of a threat from Oliver, I will personally punch you on the nose.' She scowls, then grins. 'That is a real threat.' The mischievous glint is back in her eyes. 'Promise me?'

I laugh. 'I pr-promise.'

'And *my* promise is that I will report him if he tries to do anything mean again. I have already made a good start in speaking with Mrs Adams.'

'D-deal,' I say.

'This is a good time for a game.' Maryam beams.

I don't feel like playing.

'What is it?' she says, watching my face.

I shrug.

'Shrug, shuffle, mumble,' she chides. '*Speak*, Finlay. Words are important, they mean something. Never forget they are *your words* and even if they take a little longer to get out, they are worth waiting for, yes?'

I suppose she's right. But I'm not entirely sure Maryam will want to hear them.

'Well?'

'I'm s-so sc-scared if I h-have to do a sp-speech at the ch-ch-championsh-ships,' I manage, finally.

'Finlay, get the board.'

'Huh?'

'The board.' She nods over at the coffee table.

I can't be bothered to argue. I pick up the board and look around for my tile bag.

'Just the board is fine.' She pats the seat next to her on the settee. 'Sit here.'

Just the board and no tiles?

Maryam smiles. 'Finlay, this may be your most powerful Scrabble lesson yet.'

WHEN THE TILE BAG IS EMPTY AND ONE PLAYER HAS AN EMPTY TILE RACK, THE GAME WILL END. THE WINNER IS THE PLAYER WITH THE HIGHEST OVERALL SCORE.

Maryam shuffles closer to me, so the board is resting half on her knees, half on mine.

'Look at the board,' she whispers.

I stare at the board.

Maryam looks at me and sighs as if I'm a hopeless case. 'I mean, *really* look at the board, Finlay. You are looking at life.'

I look at the plain squares, interspersed with the coloured ones. I can't say it's like *life*.

'Lots of plain, ordinary squares like the ordinary days of your own week.'

I can sort of see what she's getting at, but it still sounds a bit crazy. I imagine the empty squares filled with tiny moving pictures of me. Going to school, feeding Neville, doing my homework, playing Scrabble. Choking on stupid words.

'Every so often, a special day comes along.' Maryam's finger traces the board and lands on a deep blue triple-letter square. 'An opportunity. A way to transform the ordinary into something special, and sometimes, if you're lucky, into something that is truly amazing.'

Maryam looks at me and her eyes burn with something honest and true.

'One more move and you're on a coloured square, Finlay,' she says. 'Who knows what this amazing opportunity can bring. Please don't be afraid of being *you*, of just being who you are.'

And then she folds up the board.

After Maryam leaves, I turn off the lamps and sit for a while in Dad's chair.

Everything seems more confused and up in the air than ever. Maybe the thing to do is to clear everything from my messed-up head and start again. Like a clean board.

I *can* speak if I need to, I know I can do it. It might take three times longer than anyone else, I might turn red and nearly die of embarrassment, but the words will come out eventually, if I keep trying.

Scrabble used to take me away from my stammer troubles and even helped me forget about Mum for a little while. But lately, things have changed. Nobody can stop me achieving my goal but me. Yes, I want to win the championships to make my mum proud but for the first time, I want to feel proud of myself, too.

Speaking in public is just an ordinary square I have to pass in order to get to the exciting bit. I'm not going to let a few tricky words stop me from getting there.

Everything seems to make a bit more sense. Maybe Mum really *is* Alex's stepmum. Or not. Maybe Mum *will* see me in the press if I win the championships and get in touch. Or not.

There are no guarantees. But one thing I can be one hundred per cent certain of is that if I do well in the championships, I will be proud of *myself*. And Maryam will be proud of me, and Mrs Adams, too. And Dad. My Dad will be *really* proud.

Mum is gone. But I still have other people I care about and who care about me.

I am worth knowing and I am a good friend. Good things happen when you use your bonus squares, and right now, I feel like I'm standing right on the edge of one.

THE POINTS TOTAL FOR ANY REMAINING TILES IS DEDUCTED FROM EACH PLAYER'S FINAL SCORE.

I wake with a jolt in Dad's chair. I don't want to start sleeping down here fully clothed like him. I make sure both front and back doors are locked and turn off the rest of the lights downstairs.

My legs feel almost too heavy to climb the stairs but just a few minutes later I'm lying on my bed in my pyjamas. Wide awake.

I look over at my computer. The monitor light is winking and before I know it, I'm sitting in front of it.

Even though it's late, Alex is online.

Hey! Thought you'd ditched me ☺

No way, I say. **Was really tired but wide awake now.**

Yeah, I know the feeling. Good day?

Yeah, I type. **Apart from that idiot Oliver, giving me grief at school AGAIN!!**

How come?

I tell him about the Scrabble game and how

Oliver forced me to let him win.

He sounds like a nasty piece of work, Alex says. **The championships sound really important to you.**

I take a second to think about whether I want to get into this conversation.

It could be a way to find my mum, I confess.

There's about a minute of silence with no reply and I start to yawn and think about getting back into bed again. Then Alex comes back.

Sounds interesting. What's the plan?

I like the way Alex talks about it as if it's a problem we can solve together. I tell him about my plan to try and win the championships so that Mum has a chance of seeing me. It feels weird to be talking to him about how hard I'm trying to find my mum, when part of me is screaming, *She might be right there, with you!*

But your mum knows where to find you now, right?

We moved, I say.

I've been thinking, types Alex. **You sure she didn't leave you any clues about why she left? Sometimes clues aren't obvious, right? She could've hidden something for you to find.**

Why would she do that?

Dunno. I imagine him shrugging. **Maybe she didn't want anyone else to find it? Like your dad.**

I like Alex, but he's talking about Dad like he's part

of the reason for Mum leaving. I pull my fingers back from the keyboard. I don't like the way the conversation is going. I can feel the weight of the unknown pulling me down again.

Just trying to help, Alex sends.

Do you know when you're coming to Nottingham? I ask.

Not yet, Alex types. **Speak tomrw.** He logs off.

I sit on the floor by Neville's cage. Alex's words are running through my head like a burst water pipe: *Sometimes clues aren't obvious, right? She could've hidden something for you to find.*

'Like w-what, Neville?' I ask. 'And why?'

Neville sits on his haunches, nibbling a peanut while he watches me. He looks as though he's actually considering my question.

'Mum could've just sat me d-down and told me why she was leaving. I mean, I was t-twelve, not five.'

Neville stuffs the peanut into his cheek pouch and selects a sunflower seed.

Maybe she didn't want anyone else to find it? Like your dad. Alex's words echo in my head.

'It's ridiculous. Dad m-misses Mum as much as I do – right, Nev?'

Even though he insists that she left us without a backward glance.

Neville drops his half-eaten sunflower seed and scurries over to his water bottle, turning his back on me completely.

Like me, he's finding the whole thing impossible to work out.

IF THE PLAYER WHO ENDED THE GAME HAS NO REMAINING TILES, AN ADDITIONAL POINTS BONUS IS ADDED TO THEIR FINAL SCORE.

Friday

After showering and dressing, I head off to the supermarket to get some food in before Dad gets back from Brighton, later.

I've hardly touched the money he left for me. My jeans feel baggier around my middle and I realize I've sort of just got used to having a grumbling feeling in my stomach.

It's time to get myself back on track.

I'm looking forward to seeing Dad later and I'm thinking of getting something different in to try and tempt him away from chips and beans for once. I'm so deep in thought that I don't realize I've taken the long way round to the shops, past the youth club, until it's too late.

There's a small crowd of young people standing outside the entrance. I pull my fleece hood up, stick my hands in my pockets and stride past, hoping nobody will notice me. But what I overhear makes me grind to a halt.

'So is Oliver OK?' someone calls out.

'He's a brave lad,' a gruff voice replies. 'He'll get through it but whoever did this isn't going to get away with it.'

I see a tall, wide man in a heavy construction jacket with sandy hair and eyes the same shade of grey as Oliver's standing in the middle of the group of kids. I stop to listen to what he has to say.

'I'm asking you all to keep your eyes and ears open. If you see or hear anything about what happened to my son, anything at all, then you let me or the police know. Got it?'

Lots of mumbling and nodding of heads.

'Because whoever did this is a coward of the worst order.' The big man's voice cracks. 'My advice to you kids is to steer clear of anyone trying to talk to you or offer you money.'

Then Oliver's dad is gone, back to his truck, with a murderous look on his face.

I spot a girl from my form standing at the edge of the group.

'Wh-what ha-ha— What h-happened?' I eventually manage.

'Oliver Haywood got hit by a car.' Her eyes pop with gossip. 'It happened last night, near the entrance to the park. A bloke came up to him, saying he had an "opportunity" for Oliver to earn a bit of cash.'

'Wh-what k-kind of opp-opp—' My fingernails dig deep into my palms.

'Dunno.' The girl shrugs. 'Oliver got creeped out and ran off, but the man went mental and started chasing him. Oliver ran straight into the road and got hit by a car. He must've been really scared.'

Something stirs in my stomach and suddenly I feel quite hot. I pull down my fleece hood and smooth my hair back.

The girl's face is flush with the drama of it all. 'His dad says Oliver could've died. He's OK, but he won't be back at school for a while.'

At the supermarket I find it hard to concentrate. I suppose I ought to feel glad that Oliver has got his comeuppance. But there's something I can't put my finger on that just doesn't feel right about the whole thing.

I take the food shopping back home, put the milk and juice in the fridge. Instead of watching TV, I do some work with the anagram book that Maryam dropped off and I revise my two-letter-word lists. Then I go back into the kitchen to check the back door is locked and leave Dad a note to say I'll be back early evening.

Mrs Adams has arranged for me and Maryam to practise at the youth club, now we've broken up from school.

It's great to be able to come here for once and not have to worry about Oliver throwing his weight around. The championships are taking place in Birmingham in less than a week's time and I'm determined to really knuckle down and focus on the training.

When I arrive, I spot some of the other players from the school Scrabble club who I haven't had a match with yet. The atmosphere is relaxed and friendly.

Today, Maryam wants us to focus on *intersecting words*.

'This is where your two-letter words can really earn you some serious points.' She shows me how to scan the board quickly to see if it's possible to create a new word that will intersect with other words. 'You will earn points for any two-letter words you can create, as well as points for your new word.'

'It's l-l-like using some-s-some-one else's t-turn to your own ad-advantage.' I grin. 'Turning their words against th-them.'

Maryam's face turns more serious. 'You must also guard that someone does not do the same to you.'

Maryam has got this way of saying one thing and meaning another. There's a deeper meaning that I know is there but I can't quite grasp it.

I don't mind admitting it; sometimes Maryam gives me the creeps.

THE OVERALL WINNER IS THE PLAYER WITH THE FINAL HIGHEST SCORE.

As we walk home from the youth club, Maryam insists we play a word game, taking turns to brainstorm two-letter words.

'QI, JO, ZA.' I offer my three without much enthusiasm.

'You will thank me for this.' Maryam grins. 'When you hold up your trophy, it will all be worth it, Finlay.'

My face tingles just thinking about it. If I win, it will definitely be worth it, even with the added horror of a making a winner's speech.

I wave when Maryam turns down her street and increase my walking pace.

I'm just a few steps along our road when I spot Dad's van outside the house. I feel glad that he's home. OK, so Dad isn't the best cook, he sometimes speaks before he thinks, and at times he finishes my sentences. But at the end of it all, he's my dad.

I burst through the back door, expecting him to be

rifling through the freezer for fish fingers instead of cooking something with the fresh stuff I bought and put in the fridge. But the kitchen is empty and the TV isn't even on. Dad's boots are cast aside at the door and his fluorescent site jacket is slung over a chair.

'D-Dad?'

'Up here,' I hear him call. His voice is flat and heavy.

My head suddenly feels all stuffy but I kick off my shoes and climb the stairs.

Dad's bedroom is upside down. I mean ten times worse than before.

Mum's clothes are strewn about and I spot some of the photos from the chest scattered about the floor.

Dad sees me looking at Mum's stuff but he doesn't even try and cover it up, he doesn't say anything at all.

'W-what h-happened?' My words sound thin and choked.

'We've been done over.' Dad stands staring, his fists clenching and unclenching. 'Robbed.'

'W-why would th-thieves be interested in th-this stuff?' I say, pushing at some of the clothes with the side of my foot.

Dad doesn't answer me.

My insides pull tight as if everything has been shrunk, then stretched out again. I feel as though I'm responsible, somehow, for what has happened. Which is just stupid.

Then my head immediately empties of any thoughts

but one, and I gasp and run into my room. Neville's cage is tilted at an angle. The wire door is wide open and his little house has been upended.

Neville is gone.

While the police are asking Dad questions in the living room, I stand in the gloomy hallway, listening and watching through the crack in the door.

'Has anyone got any grudges against you that you know of?' one of the policemen asks.

'No, there's nothing,' Dad says. To the police, his voice will sound normal, but I can hear a little quiver underneath.

The taller policeman looks around the room.

'From where I'm standing, it looks as if they just wanted to mess the place up. Nice flatscreen TV over there that they didn't bother taking. What exactly *is* missing?'

It feels like someone is squeezing my heart really hard when I think about Neville.

Dad hesitates for a second or two. 'Haven't really had a chance to take a proper look, as yet,' he says.

There's a short silence and then I hear the shuffling of feet. One of the policemen coughs. 'Here's my card, sir. Give us a ring when you've had a *proper look*.' He says it like he thinks Dad is having him on.

'Best if you leave everything as it is, if you can,' the

other policeman says. 'Better for forensics, when they get here.'

I step back into the kitchen until the policemen leave and then I go into the sitting room. Dad is slumped in the chair with his elbows on his knees, resting his head in his hands.

'Who could've done this, Finlay?' he says, without looking up.

I feel like I should know the answer.

'There's nothing missing.' His words are muffled. 'I didn't want to tell the police that but I could see right away that whoever broke in didn't take anything.'

'Nev-Neville has g-gone.' I swallow down a sob.

'He's probably around here, somewhere.'

'W-why was his c-cage door open th-then? Why w-would someone d-do that?'

Dad doesn't say anything.

'Y-you don't c-care,' I burst out. 'Y-you n-never liked h-him.'

'Don't be silly, lad.'

'Mum s-said you never w-wanted her to b-buy him.'

'I didn't mind.' Dad sighs. 'I just disagreed with all that gobbledygook she'd read somewhere that a hamster could help with your stammer.'

'B-but he d-did,' I mumble. 'He d-did help.'

Dad opens his mouth and then closes it again.

I think of the way Neville looks at me through the

bars of his cage and listens. He does listen, I'm sure of it. Neville doesn't care what I speak like. The only time he doesn't take much notice is when he's pounding away on his wheel and then he doesn't notice anything, much.

I start to cry; I can't help it. I wait for Dad to tease me – *'How old are you? Fourteen or four?'* But he doesn't.

Pathetic, pathetic, pathetic, the voice in my head taunts me.

'I need a smoke,' Dad says, standing up and patting his pockets for his lighter.

'All y-you do is sm-smoke,' I snap. 'F-fag after f-flipping f-fag, every t-time you've a sp-spare m-minute.'

Dad's jaw starts twitching but he pushes the packet of cigarettes back into his jeans pocket.

'Y-you could d-die fr-from lung c-cancer, D-Dad. Th-then you'll be g-gone. L-like Mum's g-gone, like Ne-Neville's g-gone.'

'Come on now, lad,' Dad says softly. 'He'll be knocking around here somewhere, you'll see.'

'Wh-where?'

'Somewhere,' Dad says again. But he doesn't look as though he really believes it.

There are no clues to Neville's whereabouts. It's just as though he's disappeared into thin air. Or someone has taken him away, whisked him out of the house in their jacket pocket.

He could be alone and scared and even badly hurt. I squeeze my eyes shut and imagine him back in his cage, safe in my bedroom.

When I open my eyes, nothing has changed.

As the last of the sun sets, it catches on the shards of glass from the photo frame that held a picture of me and Dad on the Alton Towers log flume ride, taken three summers ago. Mum didn't want to come on the ride, so she stood and watched us as we hurtled by, whooping and waving. The scattered glass shimmers and glints, like the last bit of its life is finally flickering out.

I feel like screaming and smashing stuff up. I also feel really quiet and sad inside.

'There can only be one explanation,' Dad says, so softly I have to lean forward to catch his words.

He looks up and his hands drop from his head, down to his knees.

I don't say anything. I hold my breath and wait. Maybe Dad has thought of where Neville might be.

'I think whoever broke into the house was looking for something,' Dad whispers. 'Something I should have told you about long before now.'

ALL WORDS FOUND IN ANY STANDARD ENGLISH DICTIONARY ARE ALLOWABLE IN A GAME OF SCRABBLE.

Even though I know Dad has got something important to tell me, I can't stop moving stuff. I can't stop searching for Neville in places I know he can't possibly be.

'Finlay, there's something I need to tell you,' Dad says again. 'Sit down, lad.' He slumps forward and sinks further down into his chair.

My legs are all shaky and although I want to shout at Dad to *just – tell – me – now*, I perch on the end of the settee and sit on my hands to try and stop them trembling.

Dad runs his hand through his hair and little splinters of wood fly out. He looks up at the ceiling and down at his feet. He taps one socked foot on the floor and then the other.

'D-do you kn-know where sh-she is?' I break the silence.

'No,' Dad's head snaps up. 'Finlay, I swear.'

My whole body is aching. I wish I could just lie down

right here on the floor and sleep.

Dad looks at me, opens his mouth as if to speak and then shuts it again.

I wait.

And wait.

I don't want to know what Dad has to tell me, and yet at the same time I'm desperate to know what he's got to say. Inside my head there are tonnes of questions, all whirling around like feathers in a storm.

'Just after she left, your mum contacted me. Just the once.'

I knew it. *I knew it!*

I jump up, blood rushing to my face. 'Y-you lied! You s-said you h-h—' I stop, take a great big breath and push out the words. 'You-said-you-hadn't-heard-f-from-her.'

Dad cocks his head to one side and looks at me, surprised, then carries on talking. 'I didn't lie, I haven't heard from her since, Finlay. Since way back then, just a few days after she left.'

I can't speak.

'It was just the once, that's it.'

He's trying to play it down. He's trying to dismiss this massive, significant thing that he's kept from me all this time.

'Wh-what d-did she s-say?'

Dad reaches into his pocket and pulls something out. He closes his eyes briefly and when he opens them and raises his hands I see he is unfolding the piece of newspaper I found buried at the bottom of the wooden chest.

'She came to me on the building site I'd been working on,' he says, staring at the print. 'It was three days after she left. You were at school, and I remember I'd just sat down with a flask of hot tea and I thought she'd come back home but –'

'W-what d-did she s-say?'

'She gave me this.' He hands me the article I've already read.

I look at it for a few seconds.

'What d-does it mean?'

'You know that Bunny village is a place close to your mum's heart.'

He's babbling on. But at the same time, he's said more about Mum in the last five minutes than he's done for over two years.

Dad's face is a funny grey colour. His eyes are flitting about all over the place and I wait until they settle on my face.

I point to the eleven digits he has scrawled at the top of the page.

'The telephone number of the Post Office.' He sighs.

But, of course, I already know that.

'D-did she t-tell you w-why she l-left?'

Dad looks down at the newspaper article. His hands are shaking a bit.

'D-Dad?'

'No. I mean, I already knew why she went, I suppose . . .' He turns away and fiddles with the drawer. 'Or maybe I just thought I did . . .'

He isn't making any sense.

'S-surely she s-said *s-something*.'

'She told me if there was ever an emergency with you, strictly a life-or-death emergency only, I'm to leave a message at the Post Office in the village as she'd rented a PO Box there.'

Something powerful sweeps through me and I lean back against the wall. I feel sick and dizzy but I want to pound at Dad's chest with my fists. I take a massive breath.

'All-this-time-I-could've-contacted-Mum.' I speak until my outbreath and the words it carries dry up. 'All-th-this-time-y-you've-l-lied.'

'No!' Dad takes a step forward and reaches out to me, but I slide further along the wall and fold my arms over my chest. 'It had to be a strictly life-or-death emergency only, or she would never have responded.'

'You c-could've lied to h-her,' I cry. 'Y-you could've said I w-was ill or s-someth-thing t-to br-bring her ba-ba—'

Back. He could've thought of a thousand emergencies to bring her back.

My cheeks are all wet.

'Your mum made me promise, Finlay. I had to swear there would be no contact for any other reason at all.'

'M-maybe it was a c-cry for help,' I sob. 'M-maybe she told you be-because she *wanted* y-you to c-contact her.'

Dad shakes his head.

'If you'd have seen her eyes, you'd understand,' he says, looking down. 'She was, I don't know, *different* in some way. Her eyes were cold, like she'd put an invisible wall up around herself.'

'You sh-should have t-told me.' My voice sounds small and broken. Nothing I say will ever make a difference.

Dad walks forward quickly and pulls me into a hug before I can escape him. 'I was scared of hurting you even more,' he says into my hair. 'I wanted to protect you, Finlay.'

'F-from what?'

'I was worried she'd only break your heart again.'

'Br-break my heart, h-how?'

He doesn't answer, just closes his eyes briefly. He isn't making any sense at all. All this time, Dad knew Mum's whereabouts and never said a word.

Dad sighs. 'The Post Office arrangement proves nothing about where she actually lives now. I've been up there, asked around. She's not there, son, it's just a place she chose to touch base if it was ever absolutely necessary.'

OFFICIAL SCRABBLE DICTIONARIES ARE ALSO AVAILABLE, AND THESE ARE REGULARLY UPDATED WITH NEW, URBAN WORDS.

For four or five seconds, I press my face into Dad's shoulder and think about all the nights I've lain awake, wondering where Mum is. Worrying if she is OK, if she's safe.

I think about all the letters I've written to her in her old journal. Letters I could have posted, that she might actually have read.

I pull out of Dad's embrace and step away. My eyes are like lasers, trained on to his tired, bristly face. I've got this awful smouldering sensation like indigestion, only a hundred times worse. It burns all the way into my chest. It feels like hatred.

But I don't hate my dad.

'S-someone broke in for th-that?'

I nod to the newspaper cutting he still clutches in his hand and Neville's little face comes into my head again. I close my eyes.

'No, Finlay. They didn't break in for this.'

He sighs and sinks down into his chair.

The cutting flutters to the floor and it feels like the temperature drops suddenly in the room, but I know it's just my imagination.

'I've been getting some funny phone calls,' Dad says, his face reddening. 'On my work phone. It's been happening for a while.'

My head is whirling, the room is spinning. I try to focus on Dad's voice because I've been waiting for this moment for so long. Waiting for him to tell me the truth. And now the moment is here, I'm absolutely terrified.

But Dad doesn't seem to notice. He carries on talking. 'The caller is a man. He knows stuff about us and he knows stuff about your mum.'

'Wh-what s-sort of st-st—'

The words get stuck. I feel hot and shaky, and before I can take a breath and try again Dad answers me. 'He knows exactly when your mum left and which school you go to. I'd hoped working away would keep him focused on me and away from around here.'

Dad rubs his forehead hard with the flat of his hand.

'I know I should've told the police and I'm going to. I am. But first I needed to tell you. I need you to understand, Finlay.'

Understand? If anything, things seem more complicated than ever. Is Dad trying to say that this man is *with* Mum? Knows Mum? I'm confused.

'He says he knows I have something that your mum left behind, and that he needs it. He says if he gets it, nobody will get hurt.'

An ice-cold shiver runs through me. 'Wh-what is it th-that he w-wants?'

Dad shrugs. 'I don't know . . . and the weird thing is, he doesn't either.' Dad looks at me and stays silent until I meet his gaze. 'He says Mum got herself into some trouble with a big company. He says she stole some information and they want it back.'

I shake my head, trying to make sense of it all.

'Mum, st-steal? That's just st-stupid,' I say.

'I know,' Dad agrees. 'But he says if I get him this information they'll forget all about it. All about us. And all about her . . .'

This is all getting too big for my head to cope with.

'I need to go to the police but what do I say? I don't know for certain who this man is, who the company is. I don't know what information he's talking about, and I don't have any proper contact details for your mum. I'm pretty sure they're not going to take me seriously.'

I think about the two policemen who came out earlier and how they'd react to what they'd no doubt see as Dad's senseless ramblings.

'Y-you should l-leave Mum a m-message at the p-post o-office,' I say.

'I have,' Dad says quietly. 'It's been a few days and there's been no response.'

Dad looks pale and tired. He also looks scared.

My insides feel sore and jumbled up.

'I've tried to ignore it. I've spent a bit more time in Brighton than I've needed, trying to keep trouble away from you, but then I come back to this.' He sweeps his arm around the chaotic room, drawers turned out, furniture broken. 'I've already searched through everything we brought with us from our old house and there's nothing here. *Nothing*.'

I think about how I've heard Dad banging about upstairs, even venturing up into the loft and emptying boxes. My head flashes hot, then cold. I feel like I have a fever but I can't stay still, I need to search, I need to find whatever Mum left here. What it was she *stole*. All the work Mum did for the companies she worked for were kept in spreadsheet form. And she took her laptop with her when she left.

'I w-wonder who th-this m-man is,' I say to Dad.

'I don't know,' he says, and his face looks strange. 'I never knew what she was up to, that was part of the trouble.'

Dad's acting weird. My world feels like it's morphing out of shape. I still can't believe Mum would steal information. That doesn't sound like her at all. She was the kind of person who would go back to a shop if she discovered the cashier had given her too much change. Once, the waitress at our local pizzeria left our starters off the bill and Mum pointed out her mistake.

'What did you do that for?' Dad had grumbled. 'As if they don't make enough profit.'

'It's not the big corporations that suffer,' Mum had said, while we waited for the amended bill. 'It's the little guys who pay. Her boss will stop the shortfall from her wages.' Mum was always looking out for somebody.

'I'll c-come with you,' I say. 'To t-tell the p-police, I m-mean.'

Dad doesn't look at me. 'I need to think about what I'm going to say, first,' he says firmly. 'I need to think how I'm going to explain the situation to them when I don't even understand it myself.'

PLAYERS ARE NOT ALLOWED TO USE ABBREVIATIONS, PREFIXES OR SUFFIXES ON THE BOARD.

Saturday

I can't sleep. Soon as I start to drop off, I wake up again with a start, thinking – hoping and praying – that the tiny creak or scratch I thought I just heard is Neville.

I spend all of Saturday searching for him around the house. I look in every corner of every room and ignore Dad telling me that he'll turn up somewhere, given time. I don't log on to the computer at all. I haven't got time to chat with Alex: finding Neville is far more important.

But I do phone Maryam and tell her about the break-in, because we're supposed to meet for training at the youth club, after lunch on both Saturday and Sunday.

'Finlay, this is terrible news. Is there anything I can do to help?'

'We're just tidying round.' I don't tell her the things Dad has said about Mum. It barely makes sense to me so I doubt Maryam will be able to help.

*

Dad hasn't mentioned going back to Brighton since the break-in. When I sneaked a look at his work diary, I saw that he'd scrubbed all the jobs he had on this week, too.

I stick a couple of sugar cubes from the cupboard into my pocket and walk down to the racecourse, just to get out of the house. All up Bendigo Way, my eyes are searching every nook and cranny, just in case I spot Neville scurrying in the gutter, trying to find his way back home.

Old George is on the main gate at the racecourse, reading his paper. I've been coming here ever since we moved to our new house and Dad started doing a few odd maintenance jobs for the management company. Old George talks a lot about Nottingham Forest Football Club in their glory days and he doesn't expect much of an answer back.

I loiter around the gate until he looks up from his paper.

'Go on then, while it's quiet.' Old George rolls his eyes. 'Don't go getting into no bother back there, mind.'

I walk into the main grounds. I can hear chatter from the bar but I'm not bothered about that. I walk in a big circle until I get to the enclosures.

Back here, near the stables, there is no one around. The yard is scattered with hay and the odd pile of horse droppings, and most of the stable doors are closed. A soft snort to my left catches my attention. A glossy chestnut head appears at the half-open stable door. I reach into my pocket for the sugar cubes and hold them out on a flat hand.

'Like that do you, b-boy?' I say as he snuffles the treats from my palm, his warm breath tickling my hand. Then I lay my head against his. He stays still, as if he's listening to my thoughts. 'Mum loved horses,' I whisper. 'She w-would've loved you.'

He shifts from one foot to the other and nuzzles closer. I hope he's happy and that his owner looks after him. I close my eyes for a moment and breathe in his horsey scent.

I feel like I'm in a safe place, here. I wish I could just stay here and never go home.

Sunday

'We n-need to go to the p-police,' I say when I come downstairs on Sunday morning, to find Dad's slept in his chair all night again.

'I know,' he says without looking up. 'I'm just getting everything straight in my head, first.'

He's been trying to get everything straight in his head since the break-in on Friday. Anyone can see it isn't working.

After the forensic man left, I tidied up as best I could, but the house is still upside down and Dad hasn't touched the mayhem in his own bedroom. For two days, he's sat in the middle of all the mess, barely moving. *Thinking*, he calls it.

'You c-can't get everything st-straight in your h-head, when h-half the in-f-formation is m-missing,' I point out, but he doesn't reply.

Monday

When I come downstairs early on Monday morning, I expect to find Dad in the living room, fully clothed and unshaven again. But he's in the kitchen and his hair is damp from the shower.

'I'm cleaning up my bedroom today,' Dad says while we eat cereal together, even though neither of us is hungry. 'I know I've got to get moving on things, get things straight in the house, start throwing stuff out.'

He means getting rid of Mum's stuff. The things he said he'd already thrown away.

'I've g-got some t-time be-before I m-meet M-Maryam,' I say. 'I'll h-help you.'

Dad doesn't look very keen but I follow him upstairs anyway and stand in the doorway of his bedroom. The mess is even worse than I remembered it.

I think about Neville and I have to close my eyes to try and break up the pictures in my head. I've searched drawers and cupboards, places he could never even reach.

197

Nothing. No Neville . . . and nothing that Mum could've left behind.

I start to scratch my arms, lightly at first, then harder, but nothing seems to ease the itching.

'Finlay,' Dad says, grasping my arms gently. 'You're going to hurt yourself. Relax.'

I let my hands fall to my sides.

'Let's just get everything back in the chest for starters,' Dad suggests.

'You t-told me you th-threw all Mum's pho-photo-g-graphs and clothes aw-away,' I say quietly as I start to gather things up.

'Yes, well, I was going to,' Dad says without looking at me.

'Th-then w-why d-didn't –'

'I just didn't, OK?' Dad snaps. When he looks at me his face is red and his eyes are even redder. 'I thought – oh, I don't know. Idiot that I am, I thought she might come back one day.'

I keep my eyes on the floor, keep gathering up the photographs and setting them in small piles.

'It was the hardest thing in the world for her to leave you.' Dad sighs. 'Her face – I've never seen anyone look so torn up before.'

But she still left, I think.

We work for a few minutes, with Dad cocking his head to one side now and then, as though he's listening. 'There it is again,' he whispers after a moment or two. 'I thought I heard something.'

I stop shuffling photographs into piles and listen. I can't hear anything. Then, just as I'm about to tidy the photos away into the wooden chest, there it is: a faint scrabbling, a scraping sound coming from the other side of the wall.

'It's either rats,' Dad says, pressing his ear to the wall and grinning at me, 'or it's our Neville.'

'N-Neville!' I jump up from the floor.

Dad puts a finger to his lips. 'Quiet, now. We don't want to spook him.' He stands up straight. 'He must've got in there through here.'

He points to a small, square door in the wall leading to the attic that now stands slightly ajar. 'I was in there the other day, looking for something. I must've forgotten to close it properly.'

If it *is* Neville in the attic, he must somehow have got out of his cage – probably when the robber(s) kicked it over – and scurried along the landing into Dad's room. The attic is enormous and runs the full length of the eaves. We'll never find Neville in there; he has a million places to hide away.

'I have an idea,' says Dad. 'Wait here.'

I hear him rattling around downstairs in the kitchen and then he is back. Armed with peanuts.

'Open the attic door a bit wider,' he whispers, like he's

worried Neville might overhear him.

I do as he says, and then we lay the peanuts in a long line, leading into the middle of Dad's room.

'We'll put one or two inside the door so he gets a taste for them.' Dad winks.

He grins at me and I grin back. He seems to want to find Neville as much as I do.

Dad goes downstairs again and comes back up with two steaming mugs of tea. Then we sit on the bed and wait.

It's ages since we've just sat together without Dad reading his paper or watching TV. We're staying really quiet because we don't want to scare Neville off, but it's a nice kind of quiet.

I'm staring into space, thinking about all my problems, when Dad gives me a sharp nudge. I look at him and he nods to the attic door. Neville's tiny paws appear on the door ledge and then he pops his head up and sniffs the air. In a jiffy, he's clambered down on to the floor and is carefully packing the peanuts, one by one, into his bulging cheeks.

Soon he'll have enough in there to see him through until Christmas.

When he's moved to the fifth peanut on the trail, Dad whispers, 'I think it's safe to nab him now. Quick as you can, Finlay.'

I move like lightning and, just a few seconds later, I

have Neville's warm, furry body safely in my hands. I kiss the top of his head.

'Neville's Great Adventure!' Dad grins, marking it out as a headline in the air. 'Sounds like an action movie I'd like to see.'

We go straight to my room and I put Neville in his cage and securely fasten his door. He looks decidedly peeved that he had to leave the other peanuts behind.

'Th-thanks, D-Dad,' I say.

'You don't have to thank me, son,' Dad says, ruffling my hair. 'Neville's family. And in this family, we look out for each other, right?'

THERE IS A FLOURISHING ONLINE SCRABBLE COMMUNITY.

I'm still too early for meeting Maryam at the youth club, so I walk up into Colwick Woods and sit on a bench.

From here, I can see the sails of Green's Windmill in the distance, turning lazily in the light wind. The sun is battling to get through the thick clouds and failing miserably. I feel glad of my cosy fleece but inside I have a warm glow all of my own.

Neville is safe again.

There's hardly anyone around, just a dog walker talking on his phone and a runner who pounds by without even glancing my way. I'd like to talk to someone about the break-in and the man who's been phoning Dad, but it would be impossible getting all those words out in one piece and in the right order.

Nobody can help, anyway, because nobody knows the full story. Not even Dad.

I can't help wondering if he'll ever go to the police and what he'll say to them if he does. It seems he knows lots of little bits about Mum's disappearance but nothing solid, nothing that makes sense.

I get to the club just after ten but Maryam isn't due to arrive for another half an hour. From what I hear, Oliver is still in hospital, so he must be in a pretty bad way. Although there's nothing that would make me happier than seeing Oliver get a taste of his own medicine, I still wouldn't wish this on him.

I get a Scrabble box out of the cupboard and sit at a table in a quiet corner. Then I pull my tile bag from my rucksack and empty out the contents, turning each one face up, so I can see the letters.

I slide them around and make random words.

MYSTERY [15]

There are so many mysteries whizzing around in my mind, it's hard to separate them all out. But I have a go:

- Why did Mum leave so suddenly and without saying goodbye?
- Why would Dad say he'd destroyed Mum's stuff but secretly keep it all?
- Why is Alex so friendly online but doesn't seem to want to meet up?
- Who is Nicole? Could she really be Mum, or just some other woman who left her family behind?

• What were the people who broke into our house looking for?

Worst of all, I think that if this man, whoever he is, is willing to threaten Dad on the phone and break into our house, then what might he be willing to do . . . to Mum?

I can't sit around any longer.

I tip the tiles back into my tile bag, pick my rucksack up and walk out of the youth club.

PLAYERS ARE NOT ALLOWED TO USE WORDS THAT REQUIRE HYPHENS OR APOSTROPHES ON THE BOARD.

The next thing I know, I'm standing on Maryam's doorstep, ringing the bell. I've scared myself silly with thoughts about Mum being in danger, but Dad doesn't seem to share my fear.

A lady who has the same eyes as Maryam, and is dressed in a long tunic and headscarf, answers the door.

I start to panic. I shouldn't have just turned up like this.

'Are you Finlay?' the woman asks.

I nod.

She has a stronger accent than Maryam but her eyes dance with amusement, just the same. 'Well, I am pleased to meet you.'

I nod and smile, and shake her small, warm hand.

She stands aside and sweeps her arm back.

'I am Maryam's mother. Please, come in.'

I smile and nod again, hoping I can avoid speaking. I step inside the hallway on to a rich, mahogany, highly polished wooden floor. I look down at my scruffy trainers and bend down to untie them.

'Don't worry about your shoes, Finlay. Please, just come through. Maryam mentioned you'd had some trouble at home, I hope everything is OK?'

I give her a small smile and nod. I'm not about to tell her everything is in pieces at home. I follow her down the hallway, my eyes taking in intricate embroidered wall hangings and what look like framed, hand-printed prayers in letters and signs that I can't understand.

The air smells of polish and sweet spices, and I can hear faint strains of voices coming from somewhere inside the house.

She stops at the bottom of the stairs and calls Maryam down.

'She will be down in a moment,' Maryam's mum says. 'Please, come through to the lounge.'

I follow her into a large room with glass doors that face out on to the garden.

The television is on but muted, and in the corner of the room, a very old, wrinkly woman sits propped up with cushions, watching me like a small, hungry bird.

'Who is this?' she barks in a surprisingly powerful voice.

The old lady leans forward and Maryam's mum plumps up the cushions behind her.

'This is Finlay, Maryam's friend from school, Ammi.

She is helping him to better his Scrabble game for the championships, remember?'

The old woman mutters something and shakes her head in disapproval.

'Can I get you something to drink, Finlay?' Maryam's mum says, ignoring her.

I can't just shake my head without looking rude.

'N-no, th-thank you,' I say as quietly as possible. I glance over at the old lady but she is still muttering to herself. I wonder if Maryam has told her family I have a stammer. What on earth was I thinking, coming here?

But Maryam's mum doesn't seem to notice. 'Please, Finlay, take a seat,' she says, smiling. The old woman leans forward and looks me up and down through narrowed eyes, tutting her disapproval. I can't imagine her as a young woman, sewing sequins on to her hijab.

'He is thin like a stick,' she mutters in a very thick accent. 'You had better feed him up, Beti, before he falls down a drain.' The old lady cackles, rocking backwards and forwards, enjoying her own joke.

'*Nani!*' I look round with relief as Maryam appears at the doorway. 'Don't be so rude!' She looks at me and then scowls at the old lady. 'Sorry, Finlay, the closer Nani gets to her hundredth birthday, the *ruder* she gets.'

'*Bah!*' The old woman frowns and waves us away with a hand.

Maryam pulls my arm and we move back into the hallway.

'Ignore her.' Maryam grins. 'It is nice outside, let's go and sit in the garden.'

Maryam leads me through the kitchen, where her mum is cooking something that smells sweet and delicious.

Outside we sit on the patio, at a large wooden outdoor table. The garden is large, with mature trees and immaculate flower beds. I close my eyes and lift my face up to the sun for a couple of seconds, listening to the birdsong. The grey clouds of this morning have all but vanished.

'So you visit at last.' Maryam nudges my hand. 'To what do I owe this honour?'

'I'm s-sorry,' I say, feeling ashamed. 'I sh-should have w-waited f-for you at the you-youth c-club –'

'It is fine to practise here,' Maryam says. 'You are welcome any time, Finlay. But I must say, you do look troubled.'

The back door swings open and Maryam's mum glides outside, carrying a tray.

'Sweet tea and a treat.' She smiles at us both, and touches Maryam's head with affection, before disappearing back inside.

Maryam hands me a cup of tea. It doesn't look like any tea I've drunk before. I take a sip and it is comforting: sweet and creamy. It tastes very different to the bitter builder's brew that Dad makes.

'You like?' Maryam watches me drink, smiling.

I nod.

'It is chai, and this –' she hands me a small golden, baked ball on a china plate – 'this is my favourite sweet treat, *besan ke ladoo.*'

I take a bite and it tastes like heaven; a light, warm, almond-flavoured dough with a crisp coating. Somehow, I feel safer and calmer.

Maryam beams as I finish the treat and reach for another. I'm suddenly starving hungry.

'Ammi is a very good cook,' she says. 'But be careful of Nani. She is plotting to keep you prisoner here and fatten you up.'

Her face is deadly serious but when I give her a worried look, she bursts out laughing.

'Sorry, it is only a joke. Nani is getting –' she taps her temple – 'a little eccentric in her old age.'

Maryam's pride and love for her family shines out and a longing for Mum settles on my chest, refusing to budge. I give her a weak smile and take another sip of chai.

'So, tell me,' Maryam says. 'Everything.'

Slowly I relay the events of the past couple of days. I tell her about the break-in and about Mum's Bunny village emergency plan and Dad's conviction that Mum left something behind that someone out there seems determined to get their hands on.

I don't tell her about the mystery man who's threatened Dad and I don't tell her about the accusation that Mum's been stealing information. I don't know why. It just seems too extraordinary to wrestle with and to try and explain, when it doesn't even make sense to me.

My words choke me at first, refusing to roll out smoothly. But as I relax in Maryam's company, talking gets a little easier.

'Can you think of anything, Finlay? Anything your mum might have left behind?'

I shake my head, staring at the expanse of neat, green grass.

'Wh-what would she l-leave?'

Maryam shrugs.

'Maybe a clue as to why she left home so suddenly in the first place?'

A bird warbles in the hedgerow next to where we're sitting, clear and sweet, like it's sending a message of hope.

'I c-can't think st-straight at all,' I say. 'My m-mind is just one big m-mess.'

'I've got the perfect cure for that,' Maryam says, standing up. 'If there's one thing a game of Scrabble can do, it is to straighten out your mixed-up thoughts.'

PLAYERS ARE NOT ALLOWED TO USE WORDS THAT START WITH A CAPITAL LETTER.

The last thing I feel like doing is playing Scrabble, but I can't just turn up here at Maryam's home, expecting her to listen to all my problems and ignoring anything she wants to do.

So I open my rucksack and take out my tile bag.

Maryam comes back and sets out the board and timer on the table. Then she sets down some headphones and jacks them into an iPad.

'I want you to do something, Finlay,' she says. 'Can you put the headphones on and read this aloud, please?'

She hands me a piece of paper with a paragraph about me written on it.

'W-what is it?'

'Just do it, Finlay.' She grins. 'Read it aloud over the noise of the music. I will explain very soon.'

I sigh and put on the headphones. My ears fill with a tune that's currently top of the charts. An annoying pop song I don't like.

I'm about to ask again what we're doing this for but Maryam signals for me to read.

I pick up the paper.

'My name is F-Finlay McIntosh. I live in Nottingham and I am a Scrabble genius. I have a pet hamster called Neville and a very cl-clever friend called Maryam.'

The music stops.

I take the headphones off. I think I just read that almost without stammering.

Maryam's eyes are shining. She presses her phone screen and a recording plays back of what I just read.

'I s-sound n-nearly perfect.' I gape.

'You *were* perfect, Finlay,' Maryam says. 'When you speak against a background of music or singing, your stammer almost disappears.'

'H-how?' I say.

Maryam shrugs. 'Something to do with the rhythm, the way you're breathing. Who knows. Who actually cares? You did it!'

I did. I really did it.

'Not that you can speak with music playing all the time . . . but that's not the point,' Maryam continues. 'What matters is that it's another technique you might be able to use, and also, that you know there is nothing wrong with your voice.'

'Th-thank you,' I say, handing back the headphones. 'I n-never knew I c-could do th-that.'

I wonder if Maryam will write about this in her science project. But do I really care? It feels like I just conquered the world.

'I think we should do this more often, Finlay,' Maryam says, sweeping her hand around the garden. 'Perhaps we should create a new activity – *Extreme Scrabble*, played outdoors.'

She slides over my tile rack.

'Why d-did you st-stop pl-playing Scrabble?' It's something I've often wondered.

'My uncle loved the game and taught me to play when I was very young. When he saw I had a talent, he entered me into competitions where I began to win against kids nearly twice my age. The whole family got so excited, I just sort of got carried along with it for a while.'

'D-do you m-miss playing?'

'Not really.' Maryam smiles. 'I am happy to be following my own dreams. I am proud I achieved a good level with the game, but it was never something I wanted to do for the rest of my life.'

I nod, understanding. Maryam picks up my tile bag from the table by the drawstring and rotates it so it catches the light.

Mum's embroidery looks really beautiful out here in the sunlight. I've only ever looked at it indoors and if I'm honest, I've had it so long now that I stopped noticing the intricacy of her stitches some time ago.

'So pretty,' she breathes. 'Your mum was a clever lady.' Coloured threads intertwine and catch the fabric in a thousand different ways, forming complicated geometric shapes that transform the plain cream muslin cloth underneath. 'Did she give it to you before she left?' Maryam asks.

I nod. I reach for the bag so I can make my letter selection, but Maryam empties all the tiles out on to the table and flattens the bag in front of her, loosening the drawstring so the bag is a perfect square again.

'W-what are you d-doing?'

'Just looking.'

I can hear kids squealing and laughing in the garden next door, chasing each other, but I can't see them because of the high hedges.

'Interesting,' I hear Maryam murmur.

I watch her run her fingertip backwards and forwards over the glinting silver initials 'FM' that Mum embroidered on the bag for me. I feel a bit guilty for not appreciating it enough. These days, I barely look at the bag any more.

Maryam taps her fingernail on the initials. 'There is something under here,' she says. 'You can feel it.'

I reach over and press my fingertip on the lettering. There is a small square of something, flat and hard underneath the stitches.

'Have you never noticed this before?' Maryam asks.

I shake my head. It's probably just something Mum put in so the material lies flat and the initials show up better.

'I am not surprised it has escaped your notice. On a bag filled with tiles, it would be virtually invisible to spot,' Maryam says, almost to herself.

'M-maybe she left it in by m-mistake,' I offer.

Maryam shakes her head. 'Your mum would have known it was there when she sewed the initials.'

She gets up without saying anything and disappears into the house.

I pick up the tile bag and pinch around the stitches. It feels like a tiny, hard square of plastic directly under my initials.

'Finlay, do you trust me?' She holds up a tiny pair of scissors. 'These are very sharp and precise. I could make a tiny slit on the inside of the bag, to extract whatever is there. It will not spoil the bag and no one will ever know.'

I don't know about cutting into Mum's bag: I don't want to spoil it.

'Afterwards, I can sew it up again with the tiniest stitches you can imagine.'

She opens up the empty bag and shows me the piece of inside lining she wants to snip.

'OK th-then,' I agree. It's just a bit of plastic, I don't know what she's expecting.

I watch as Maryam sticks out her tongue in

concentration and begins to snip at the fabric, before I hear a sharp intake of breath. The tile bag falls from her hands and she holds something up in the air. I shade my eyes from the sun and hold my palm out flat as Maryam places the object in my hand.

It is a tiny black square of plastic with a metal edge.

A memory card.

PLAYERS ARE NOT ALLOWED TO USE FOREIGN WORDS WHEN PLAYING SCRABBLE IN THE ENGLISH LANGUAGE.

When I get back home, Dad's van is gone. I keep calling his work mobile but it goes straight to voicemail each time. He's probably been called out on an emergency job.

It took me ages to get away from Maryam. She pleaded to come back with me to speak to Dad about our discovery but I managed to convince her that he and I needed a bit of time together to sort our heads out. She doesn't know Dad. He'll do his nut if he knows I've got other people involved in our problems.

I run upstairs and slip the memory card into my computer. After a few seconds, a new driver begins to load. It seems painfully slow. Every second feels like a full minute and the buzzing sound in my ears seems to grow louder with each moment.

Finally, the screen springs into life.

A logo I haven't seen before – three intertwined letters, 'MKF' – flashes up and is swiftly replaced by a black box containing two blank white rectangles, labelled *Username* and *Password*.

I enter various combinations: CHRISTA and FINLAY, CHRISTA and PASSWORD, CHRISTA and PASSWORD123, and about a thousand more guesses.

Not one of them opens the program.

I bang the top of my desk with my fist. I need to think hard because this is important, *really* important.

Mum went to the trouble of concealing this memory card in the most ingenious way possible. It's almost as though she didn't even want *me* to find it. The stuff on there must be pretty top secret.

Maybe, one day, she intended coming back for it. I like the thought of that.

I flip the memory card out and place it safely on my bookshelf. Then I log on to the Scrabble online portal and wait.

I distinctly remember Alex telling me he's a bit of an IT whizz. What if he can help me to crack Mum's password? It's worth a try.

Five minutes later, Alex logs in. It's amazing, he always seems to know whenever I'm online.

Hey Finlay. Long time, no speak, he types.

I don't waste any time.

I found something, I say. **I was looking for clues as to why Mum left. And I found something.**

What? What did you find? Alex pings back immediately.

A memory card but it needs a password. I wondered if

Then Alex cuts in:

You need to get that memory card to me right away.

I'm grateful Alex seems willing to help out, but this new, urgent tone is a bit startling.

That's why I came online, to ask you if you've got any tips on breaking the password, I say.

Don't meddle with it. I'll meet you in town in an hour to pick it up.

This is crazy. Alex is acting as if the memory card belongs to *him*.

I type my reply quickly.

Thanks but I don't want you to take it away, just help me to crack the password, I type. **Me and Dad will have to take it to the police.**

What he says next nearly knocks me off my chair.

If you don't want to get hurt, you'll meet me and bring the memory card with you. Understand?

I feel like I'm going to be sick. I really wish Dad was here. I suddenly feel very unsafe and nervous.

Is this Alex?

Maybe someone has logged on as Alex, pretending to be him.

Yes, this is Alex. You need to give me the memory card, do you understand?

I press my hand on my chest to try and slow my heartbeat.

I don't understand what's happening here and yet part of me does. I've put my faith in a complete stranger. How come Alex is suddenly here in Nottingham when he said he didn't know when he'd be visiting? Has he been here all along?

I'm reaching for the mouse to log off when another message flashes up.

Finlay, I'm sorry. I didn't mean to snap at you like that.

Everyone knows that other users can easily adopt a persona they want you to believe is them. I try to think for a moment.

Look, something happened today, something bad, Alex types. **Would you meet up with me to talk about it?**

He sounds normal again.

But I really don't want to get involved with his personal problems. I have enough of my own to deal with.

See, I didn't tell you the whole truth . . . there's something you need to know, Alex types. **It's about your mum. I've found something out that means she might be in danger and you might be, too.**

This doesn't sound like you, I send straight back.

My breathing comes in short, sharp bursts and my

220

hands are shaking. I feel hope, dread. Mostly, I feel sick. What does he mean about me and Mum being in danger?

I swear it's me, Finlay. I had to be horrible to make you listen – I didn't think you were taking me seriously. Please, meet me at the coffee shop at the end of your road in an hour.

How come you're suddenly in Nottingham? I ask.

We came up last night, Dad has an urgent job on. I was gonna message you to meet up anyway and then you beat me to it. I'm worried about you, Finlay, that's all.

I suppose that *could* make sense at a push. And I almost feel bad now, when Alex seems to only have my interests at heart.

Why do you think my mum might be in danger? I type. **Shall I ring the police?**

No! It could make everything worse. Let's crack the memory card code together and then I can tell you everything.

He definitely sounds like Alex again and it feels good that he seems to really want to help me, even though I feel nervous about the fact that he says Mum and me might both be in danger.

Now we're finally going to meet up, Alex will find out about my stutter but I can't hide it forever. However much I hate it, it is a part of me and it will probably always be there.

I've still got a lot I want to say.

Somehow, I'm not sure why, I think that Alex will understand. And more importantly, I need to know what he has to tell me about Mum.

OK, I say. **Meet you at the coffee shop I told you about before at the end of Bolton Grove. You take the main road out of Colwick and**

I know where you live, he interrupts before I've even finished typing my message.

I feel a chill at the back of my neck. Unconnected events start to move around in my head, sliding slowly towards each other like random tiles on the board that eventually line up to make a word.

I feel like there's something really obvious I'm not seeing yet. I'm not joining up the letters in the right way.

You told me, remember? Alex continues. **You said you lived just up the hill from the coffee shop.**

I did. I did say that. I breathe a sigh of relief.

Alex seems to know Nottingham pretty well, even though he hasn't visited much – but I guess with Google Earth and online maps, you can pretty much see where anybody lives.

I *need* to know what he knows about Mum. If my mum lives with him and his dad it would be crazy. But in some weird way, maybe it would make us almost like . . . brothers, or something.

I shake my head to stop my brain running away with all these mad ideas.

OK, I say. My heart is pounding and I can hardly swallow, my mouth is so dry, but I have to say it. My fingers fly over the keys, pushing out the words before I change my mind: **Meet you in an hour. Bring a photo of your family and I'll bring one of mine.**

I'm electrified and terrified about the idea of finding out the truth at last.

Fantastic! he sends back instantly. **And Finlay** . . .

I'm already moving away from the computer to get my journal. But I reach back and type with one hand.

Yes?

Don't forget to bring the memory card!

Monday, 25 May
Dear Mum,

I'm meeting Alex in one hour but I have to write this down to get it out of my head. It feels the whole world is going mad – the house broken into, Dad admitting you contacted him after you left, Alex acting weird . . . and now the MEMORY [13] card.

You hid it so carefully, as if you didn't want anybody to find it at all, even me. It's torture knowing that tiny plastic card holds information you wanted to keep safe. Did you write me a letter explaining why you left, and save it on there, thinking I'm cleverer than I am, and that I'd find it well before now?

I've tried everything to try and crack the password but I've had no luck at all. I'm hoping Alex will be able to help me. He says there's something he needs to tell me.

About you.

Maybe you made a mistake? Maybe you thought you wanted a new family, or got into trouble at work?

Whatever happened, Dad would have you back here tomorrow, I really believe that.

I can't help wondering if you left other clues, too. I can't IMAGINE [10] ever getting to the bottom of it all. But I'm going to try.

Love,

Finlay x

SCRABBLE IS AVAILABLE IN
TWENTY-NINE LANGUAGES.

Fifty minutes later I arrive at Coffee 'n' Cream, the cafe at the bottom of our road. It's quite busy, but there are still some free seats.

There are no lads already in there who are sitting on their own, so I choose a table tucked away in the corner from where I can see the door clearly. I imagine Alex to be a bit taller than me, someone who looks as though they've got a lot of self-confidence.

I don't know why I think that. Alex says he hasn't got many friends but I never imagine him as being lonely. It must be something to do with the way he talks and the things he says. I feel confident that I'll know him when he walks in.

I tap my hand on the edge of the table, watch a plump baby in a pushchair dribbling and squealing in delight at his own fingers, stare out of the window at an old tramp shuffling by, pushing a wonky shopping trolley piled up with all his worldly goods.

My skin starts to itch. My hands move to my arms but I force them back down again. If I can relax a little, the itching will disappear on its own. I glance at my watch again, it's ten past six and still no sign of Alex.

I look around at the tables. Mums and pushchairs, a businessman, an elderly couple, and a girl about my age sitting on her own. She looks over just as my eyes settle on her. A second of eye contact then we both look away again. I sigh and look back out of the window. I dip my fingers into the inside pocket of my denim jacket, just to make sure it's still in there.

Something makes me look across the room again. The girl is watching me and this time she doesn't look away.

She has mousy brown lank hair and a pale, thin face. She's probably about fourteen or fifteen, but she has shadows under her eyes that make her look older, tired. I want to stop looking but I can't. She's standing up. She's coming over.

Alex is going to be here any moment and it's all going to get complicated.

The words will stick together in my throat if I try to explain that I'm waiting for a friend.

'Hello,' she says. She nibbles her nails and then snatches them out of her mouth like an invisible person is telling her to stop.

She sits down in the empty seat opposite me.

'Are you Finlay?'

It feels like my cheeks are bathing the whole cafe in a rosy glow.

I start to cough and I can't stop.

'Fancy a coffee?' she says, and before I can answer, she stands up. I want to call her back, explain I'm meeting someone, but it's too late, she's at the counter, picking change out of her purse to pay for the drinks.

I glance at my watch; it's a quarter past six.

Where the hell is Alex? How does that girl know my name? I've never seen her at school or at the youth club.

A few minutes later she's back, holding two regular lattes. 'I got sugar,' she says, piling a few sachets up in the middle of the table. 'Just in case.'

I don't touch the coffee and neither does she.

She keeps shifting around in her seat, eyes darting around the cafe. Now she's chewing her nails again.

'I – I –'

I'm meeting someone: I see the words dancing tantalizingly in front of my eyes. I try again.

'I – I'm m-mee—'

The words won't come. My heart is hammering, I feel hot and out of breath. Alex will arrive any second and my stutter will be ten times worse than ever.

She looks at me.

'Are you meeting someone?' she says. 'Someone called Alex?'

I nod. I don't know how she knows all this stuff, but

hopefully she'll leave me alone now.

'Alex is here,' she says.

I look around the cafe but there's still nobody who fits his description.

'*Here*, silly,' she says, jabbing her own forehead. 'I'm Alex.'

PLAYERS ARE NOT ALLOWED TO ATTEMPT TO FEEL THE TILES IN THE BAG IN ORDER TO GUESS THE LETTERS.

My jaw drops open but Alex seems unfazed. She tears open a sugar sachet and empties it into her drink.

'Y-you're A-Alex?'

'Well actually, I'm *Alexandra*,' she says matter-of-factly. 'Alexandra King. But everyone calls me Alex.'

My head is about to explode. With heat, with panic . . . with pure embarrassment. I've been pouring my heart out to a *girl* called Alexandra?

I decide I want to die. Right here, right now.

'What's wrong with your face?' she asks. Then she grins. 'Oh, I see, you thought I was a *boy*.'

I don't smile back.

'Don't give me the evil eye, Finlay. I never said I was a boy, you just assumed it.'

That's the worst thing about it. I did. Early on, I'd pictured Alex as a boy who I might become mates with, and that was it. As far as I was concerned, Alex was male. But somehow, I can't stop feeling really angry at her.

It's like she knew I'd made that mistake and hadn't said anything. If she'd told me her full name – Alexandra – there would have been no misunderstanding.

All those thoughts are quickly swept aside as I remember that 'Alex' has finally brought the proof I've been waiting for.

'D-did you bring a ph-photograph of y-your f-fa-family?'

She shakes her head.

I bang my fist on the table and Alex's coffee wobbles in its cardboard cup, throwing a bit of milk froth over the edge.

'Whoa!' she says, reaching for a napkin. 'Calm down, Finlay. I forgot, OK? It's no big deal.'

If she knew my heart felt like a cold stone split in two, she'd know how big a deal it was. 'Y-you said you h-had s-something to t-tell me ab-about my m-mum,' I manage.

'I have but . . .' She sighs and looks at her hands, then glances around the cafe. 'Look, can we go for a walk, or something? I really need to talk to you, but not here. Let's go to the park.'

I'm *devastated*. It's the only word I can think of to give the terrible disappointment inside me a name. Finding out from Alex if her stepmum is *my* mum feels like some kind of bait she's keeping from me, something which means I'll follow her anywhere as if I'm a starving

230

rat, hoping for a few morsels to stay alive.

Colwick Park is just a five-minute walk away from where we're sitting now. Again I wonder how Alex knows Nottingham so well, but as I managed to get her gender completely wrong, who knows what other stuff has passed me by?

I wanted to believe stuff so badly, it's like I brainwashed *myself*.

We leave our untouched drinks on the table and walk in silence until we get into the park and find a bench overlooking the largest lake. A group of ducks approach us hopefully but waddle away grumbling to themselves when they see we have no food to offer.

Alex keeps looking around her, constantly twisting a piece of hair and chewing her inside cheek, but there's nobody else around, apart from a couple of dog walkers over the other side of the lake.

'I'm really sorry I lied to you, Finlay,' she says, looking out across the water. 'I didn't want to, honestly. I just – well, I hadn't really got a choice.'

'L-lied?' Although it annoyed me to admit it, she didn't actually *lie* to me about being a boy.

'I mean, it wasn't always just me you were talking to online. My dad, he . . .' She looks around again. 'He made me do it.'

Her dad made her do what? I just want to know what she knows about my mum. I can't find out what I need to know by staying silent. I know I have to speak. My words are all mixed up in the wrong order, but they're really, really important.

'D-do you kn-kn—' I swallow hard, take a big, deep breath. 'Do-you-know-my-m-mum?'

When she looks away and shakes her head, a flood of fury shoots through me. I've got this overwhelming urge to push her off the bench and walk away. She is playing some kind of stupid, cruel game with me. Everything she's said has been a temptation, keeping me logging on, going back, desperate for more information. Now I'm pressing her for the truth, she doesn't know what to say.

But that's not the real reason I'm angry. I'm furious because I've been a stupid, naive idiot who believed every last lie she fed me online. She knows nothing about my mum. She's not my friend. She never will be and she never was.

As I stand up I feel hollow inside, as if not even a shred of hope is left inside me.

'Do you have the memory card, Finlay?' Her voice is like a distant echo. I don't even really understand what she's saying, what she's asking me.

A man and a little boy have arrived and are feeding the ducks, off to my right. Most of the ducks are waddling around, happily eating the bread, but one bullying duck is stalking the others angrily, trying to bite and push them out of the way so he can eat all the bread. When

232

he finally chases the others away and looks round, all the bread has gone.

I've wasted so much time believing there is a link to Mum through 'Alex'. I've been a complete idiot.

'Just give me the memory card and I'll go away,' she says. Her voice is shaking and her face looks paler than ever. She looks around the park constantly, even turning to look behind her.

'Y-you s-said you kn-knew my m-mum,' I say, forcing the words out with more difficulty than ever. 'Wh-why?'

Alex buries her face in her hands. 'It's not me that knows her. It's my dad.' Her hands drop away, and she looks so scared and upset that if I wasn't so angry, I might actually feel a bit sorry for her. 'Your mum did some work for my dad's company, MKF . . . in Leicester.'

MKF. The logo that flashes up when I load the software.

'He hired your mum to sort out his databases while he was working on some project for the council. She was supposed to just transfer the information from one system to another, but she found something she wasn't supposed to see.' Alex's eyes harden for a second. 'Dad says she could have just ignored it, but that she had to go and stick her nose in.'

She twists round to fully face me. Two hot red spots have appeared on her cheeks and her lips look thinner, twisted. 'We lost *everything* because of your mum. Dad had to wipe his records, pull out of the contract and lie low in case your mum went to the police. We lost our *house*, and Dad became . . . well, even worse than he was before.'

My heart is pounding. This feels like a story she's making up about Mum.

Alex twists her hands into her sleeves. 'There's some kind of inquiry happening at the council that goes back six years in time. And this digital forensic expert claims that a copy of the original database was taken before it was wiped. If they find that data they're going to throw the book at Dad. He'll go to prison. Do you understand?' Her eyes take on a haunted look. 'Your mum's the only person who could have made that copy. Dad found you . . . made me start up a conversation. Turns out you were pretty easy to google. I don't know why, but for some reason Dad's convinced your mum didn't take the data with her.'

'Wh-why d-didn't you j-just say n-no?'

Alex lets out a bitter laugh. 'You don't say no to my dad, he doesn't like it.' She pushes up her jacket sleeve to rub at her pale forearm and I glimpse a row of small bruises, like fingerprints on her skin.

I keep getting a whiff of freshly cut grass and the slightly stagnant smell off the lake when the breeze blows past us. I can hear the faint hum of the council's ride-on mower in the distance. All of it seems unreal.

'That was him, earlier, online, before I took over again,' Alex says, her voice shaking. 'He knows, Finlay. Knows you have the memory card.' She glances around the park again. 'He'll do *anything* to get it back.'

'Wh-what's on it?'

Alex shakes her head. 'I don't know. Something about council house waiting lists. He'd – well, if you knew my dad you wouldn't be surprised – he'd got some kind of scam going.'

'A-and my m-mum f-found out?'

Alex bites her lip and nods. 'It was something to do with the people who were supposed to be living there. They weren't real.'

'Fr-fraud,' I said faintly.

'I heard Dad talking to his business partner about it. They'd rigged it so if your mum went to the police, it would look like she was to blame. The only real evidence that could link them to anything was on the original database. He didn't know she had a copy until now,' Alex says, looking around the park again. 'Give me the memory card and he'll leave you alone. Please, Finlay. You seem like a nice lad. I don't want anything bad to happen.'

THE TWO HIGHEST-SCORING LETTER TILES ARE 'Q' AND 'Z'.

Suddenly Alex gasps out loud and I jump up from the bench. Her eyes are wide and staring. 'No, no, no,' she whispers, her face deathly pale.

I twist round to see ducks, geese and a wide expanse of the lake, curving off to our right-hand side. And then I spot something else: a big, angry-looking man with a red face and shaved head, striding towards us. He's over six feet tall and very broad across the shoulders.

'Dad, leave it, please,' Alex calls out. Finlay's going to give me the –'

I don't wait to hear the rest. I start to run.

'Finlay, wait!' she shrieks behind me, but I don't look back. I pound, fast as I can, towards the thick copse over the far side of the lake. He's running after me. I can hear his feet scuffling, his gasping breath some way behind. I swerve to avoid a group of terriers, excited by the chase. They gather around my feet yapping, and I have to be really careful not to trip over them.

I break free and a few seconds later hear Alex's dad swear. One of the dogs yelps and its owner yells angrily. When I finally reach the wooded area, I'm gasping for breath as I launch myself in amongst the trees.

I know these woods pretty well. I jump down into a hole in the ground that local kids sometimes use as a den, and hastily pull some bracken over myself.

Then I sit still and listen, my heart bouncing off my ribcage.

Within seconds, I hear him enter the woods, panting and cursing. 'I'll find you, you little swine, and when I do, I'll wring your bloody neck.'

I hunch deeper into the hole as his footsteps come closer.

Stay still, don't breathe, I tell myself as I squeeze my eyes shut.

He stops, still for a moment. He's so close to the den I can hear him breathing. Then there is crunching underfoot again and I nearly collapse with relief. He's stomping off in the wrong direction. I open my eyes and flex the tense muscles in my neck and shoulders.

And then I hear him coming back.

He's smashing through the bracken, beating the ground with a big stick. Then he's standing right over me, and when he steps forward, his foot slips down into the den and he loses his balance.

I spring up and try to clamber out before he can catch

his breath, but a big meaty arm flies out and grabs my ankle. 'Not so fast,' he growls.

I yelp as he yanks hard on my leg and I slide back down into the hole with him. He rights himself and grabs me around the neck.

'Hand it over, you little runt.'

I can barely breathe, never mind speak. Words dance around in front of my eyes, taunting me.

'P-please,' I squeak.

'Dad, let him go!' Alex stands over us, hands covering her mouth. 'Finlay, please, just give him the memory card.'

He loosens his grip very slightly on my throat.

'I ha-ha—'

'Spit it out you idiot,' he hisses.

'Ha-haven't g-got i-it.'

'You little liar.' He bares his teeth and his face grows so red I'm sure his head is going to explode any second. 'You told her you were bringing it with you.'

'I l-left it a-at h-home,' I manage.

'Finlay, you have got it,' Alex says sadly. 'It's in your jacket pocket; you've been patting it the whole time you've been with me. Just give it to him, please, then he'll leave you alone.'

Before I can stop him, her dad plunges his hand into my pocket and pulls out the piece of folded paper I put in there before I left home.

'Hi Alex, I have a stutter. Sorry if it takes me some time to speak.' He laughs out loud, screws it up and throws it to the ground.

Alex reaches for the note. She unfolds it and reads it, but she doesn't laugh. She looks tired and drained and the shadows beneath her eyes seem darker than ever.

'I w-was checking I h-had the n-note,' I say.

'You stupid little prat,' the man snarls at me. He pushes his massive face close to my ear until I can feel his hot, sour breath on the side of my face. 'Empty your pockets, now. All of them.'

I try to do what he says but my hands are trembling and he won't wait. He starts patting me down, like an American cop, but he's hitting rather than patting, pushing his fingers roughly into my pockets. When he finds nothing, he shoves me hard against the side of the den.

I feel small and weak. And completely hopeless.

'You're a stubborn little swine, just like your mother. I don't know why I ever trusted her. I *knew* there was something in that house.'

'It was y-you that b-broke in?' I force out.

'Oh, you're so s-smart,' he mocks. 'Work out who scared that stupid kid Oliver nearly to death, too? You should be thanking me for that.'

'W-why would y-you do th-that?' I whisper.

'He did it to himself, the imbecile. I offered him cash

for information – where you lived, that kind of stuff. Not my fault he ran off when he realized I wasn't gonna pay up. Said he was going to *tell his Daddy* on me. I don't think he realized who he was dealing with.'

I feel a cold fear creeping up my spine as I realize just how far he is prepared to go to get what he wants.

'Wh-where is my m-mum?'

'How should I know?' He pushes me so hard I crash into the den wall. 'I gave the stupid cow two choices and she took the hard one.'

'Y-you *made* her l-l-leave?'

He stands tall, brushing bracken bits from his clothing. 'Like I said. She *chose* to go. Obviously didn't care enough about you and your old pa to stick around.'

It hurts as much as if he'd beaten me around the head with that heavy stick he's carrying. Alex steps forward, but he jabs the stick straight at her and she immediately takes a step back. He turns back to me. 'Your mum had the chance to make an absolute packet and be happy. But she chose to screw over every single one of us and leave instead. Happy now, kid?'

I look at his ugly, bloated face and I feel sick. On a mad impulse, I snatch the gnarled stick out of his hand and swing it up high, bringing it down hard on his fat, bald head.

He lets out a great roar and bends over, cradling his skull. When he looks up baring his teeth at me, I can see blood running down his face where the stick has scraped his scalp. He must think his head is split right open, judging by how he's bawling like a big kid.

'Run!' I hear Alex scream.

And before I know it, I'm up and out of the den and running like my life depends on it.

Maybe it does.

THERE ARE OVER A HUNDRED TWO-LETTER WORDS ALLOWABLE IN SCRABBLE.

I run down our road and feel a flood of relief as I see Dad's van is parked outside. I fall through the door, gasping and coughing as Dad jumps up out of his chair.

'Finlay! What's wrong, why –'

'Wh-where w-were you?' I cry, bending over with my hands on my knees to catch my breath. 'Y-you w-wouldn't answer y-your ph-phone.'

'I was on a job.' He grabs my shoulders and shakes me gently so I look at him. 'I left the phone in the van by mistake. What's up?'

'L-lock the d-doors,' I urge him.

'What's all this about, son?'

'J-just d-do it,' I say. 'Pl-please.'

Dad's eyes widen and he swallows hard but he does as I ask and when he comes back in the living room, I tell him everything.

All of it. From the beginning.

I tell him about first meeting 'Alex' online, and

finding the photographs and the Bunny village clipping in the chest in his bedroom. Then I tell him about finding the memory card, and finally about Alex and the clash I'd just had with her dad in the park.

'Bloody hell, Finlay,' Dad says, his mouth open.

I suddenly feel cold and really tired.

'Wait here, I'll bloody well sort that thug out,' Dad grunts, pulling on his work boots.

'N-no, Dad. W-we h-have to t-tell the police, right n-now. Mum c-could be in d-danger.'

Dad just looks at me. He opens his mouth to say something but only a sigh comes out.

'W-what?' I'm losing patience with him. 'W-what were you g-going to say?'

'I don't know,' Dad says sadly. 'I just want to punch that bully for what he's done. I've never seen him in the flesh but your mum and him, well . . .'

Dad doesn't finish his sentence.

My face feels clammy. Alex had said something about her dad having an affair. I thought it was just more lies but Dad's expression is saying something different.

'D-did M-Mum l-leave you for h-him, D-Dad?'

Dad shakes his head and sits down. He looks at his feet. 'I don't think so.' He seems to shrink a bit in front of my eyes. His broad shoulders round in on themselves and his mouth droops down at the corners. 'There was definitely something going on between them at one point. Her and

King.' He spits the name like it tastes bitter. He looks at me then. 'I'm sorry, son, I should've talked to you about this stuff a long time ago, but the longer time went on, the harder it got.'

My mind is reeling. *Mum and King?* How could she even think about being with that animal?

'T-tell me n-now!' I shout.

'You know everything, son. In fact, you know more now than I've known all this time.' Dad runs his hands through his hair and gives a heavy sigh. 'Your mum told me that King, although I didn't know his name at the time, had threatened to tell me about their affair so she'd decided to come clean about it. She said it was the biggest mistake of her life. She said he'd fooled her into believing he was a decent man. Then she said she was leaving – not to be with him, just leaving – and I asked her to . . . I asked her to leave you out of it.'

I feel hot and twisted up inside. 'W-what? Y-you h-had no r-right –'

'Finlay,' Dad booms, drowning out my fractured words. 'I did what I thought was best for you, lad. You'd only just turned twelve years old, for goodness sake, I wanted to let you down gently.'

'B-but you n-never sp-spoke to me ab-about M-Mum leaving a-at all.'

'I wanted to,' he said sadly. 'But it was never the right time.' A few seconds of silence and then Dad stands, pulling himself up to his full height. His mouth isn't drooping any more, his jaw is set and his eyes dark.

'I should've tackled King long before now. I should've hunted him down and confronted him when your mum left. I'm ashamed I just accepted her decision blindly instead of fighting to keep my family together.' An expression of pure suffering flits across his face. 'I could strangle him with my bare hands for what he's just done to you. I'm ringing the police now, before I do something I'll really regret.'

Dad picks up the phone.

'I'm sorry, lad, I shouldn't have dithered. I should've dealt with this way before now.'

I leave Dad with the phone and race up to my bedroom, hunting around in my desk drawer for the envelope of Scrabble photographs that Mum left.

Somewhere between writing Mum's letter and running home from the park, an idea has crystallized in my mind and I need to test it out. Those pictures are the only things she left me. Those and the tile bag.

There are seven photographs, all printed out on ordinary paper and all depicting games we'd played in the last couple of weeks before Mum left. I've never really looked at them properly before now. I pick up one and study it. Mum played a great word, T-R-A-N-Q [14], on her first turn. I remember challenging her, saying that there was no such word, but of course, she found it in the Scrabble dictionary and waved it in my face.

Suddenly I feel a flutter of possibility. I'm so relieved that I decided to meet up with Alex first, *before* I trusted him with Mum's precious secrets. I take the memory card from its hiding place on my book shelf and insert it into my computer.

THE LONGER WORDS ARE
NOT NECESSARILY THE
HIGHEST-SCORING WORDS.

The letters 'MKF' flash up and then disappear, leaving the empty log-on boxes. I enter Mum's name and then 'TRANQ' as the password.

Incorrect. Try again.

I pick another word. PODGE [10]. This one was one of Mum's favourites; it's what she used to call me when I was little. I tap in the letters and press enter.

Incorrect. Try again.

I let out a groan of frustration and look back at the photos, willing a word to stand out from the others. For the first time, I notice the top photograph is numbered with a small, black handwritten number '3', in the left-hand corner. I pick it up and scrutinize it.

Nothing special about it. I try one or two of the words on that sheet, but nothing works.

I spread out the photographs on my bed in a fan shape and see that each one has a tiny, handwritten number in the top left-hand corner. I nearly shout to Dad to come upstairs but decide against it. It doesn't mean anything yet and the police are on their way. It's my last chance to make sense of everything and there's no time to lose.

It occurs to me that Mum might've just numbered the games in the order we played them. But that theory is soon disproved because I distinctly remember our last game together and that one is only numbered '2'. I'm just about to gather the papers up, before the police get here, when something else catches my eye. A single Scrabble letter in the top left square of the board, disjointed and separate from the other words. Even stranger, I see there is one on every single photograph.

On sheet number 2 it's an 'A', on number 4 it's an 'S', and number 7 has an 'L'.

Will they make a seven-letter word?

My hands are shaking a little but I place the photographs in line, in numerical order, and say the letters out loud.

'W-A-L-S-A-L-L'

Walsall? I've heard of *Warsaw* in Poland, but I'm not sure where Walsall is. I think it might be a football team. I type the word into Google and discover it is a town eight miles north-west of Birmingham.

'Finlay!' Dad's shout makes me nearly jump out of my skin. 'Coppers have just pulled up.'

'C-coming!' I shout back.

I type the word 'WALSALL' into the password box and the screen jumps into life. The company logo appears again and the whole monitor fills with some kind of code. My heart seems to hammer in time with the flashes of html. When it all clears, I'm left with a small list of database files, labelled 'MKF Tenancies 1–150'.

Evidence that can put Alex's dad in prison.

They send different policemen to the two who came before. They listen carefully to everything Dad tells them and take notes. They seem to understand when Dad explains that we don't know exactly who Alex and her dad are.

'I knew Christa seemed to be getting close to the guy she worked for . . .' Dad takes a strangled breath. 'But I'm guilty of turning a blind eye. I threw myself into work and pretended there wasn't a problem.' He squirms in his seat and I can see his fingernails digging into his palms.

This is so hard for him, but he's doing it.

'We'd all act differently with the benefit of hindsight, sir,' the younger policeman says kindly.

'We should be able to trace him through our colleagues in the Leicestershire force,' the older policeman says. 'Our priority will be to make sure the girl, Alex, is safe.'

I tell them that King admitted he was the one who scared Oliver so much he ran into the road and was hit by a car. And I give them the memory card. I write down the username and password on a separate piece of paper.

'Don't worry, son, we'll take good care of it,' the younger policeman says, taking it from me and popping it into a self-sealing plastic bag. 'I'm sure our digital team will appreciate you managing to crack the password. Might even offer you a job.'

When the police have left, I feel strangely deflated. I ask Dad about the significance of Walsall but he shrugs his shoulders. 'It's not a place your mum ever mentioned to me,' he says, rubbing his whiskery chin. 'I know it's hard, lad, but try not to put too much stock on it meaning anything; it was probably just the first thing she thought of at the time.' He puts the television on, turns the sound down to mute and stares blankly at it.

My insides crackle like heated-up popcorn. I feel like we should be *doing* stuff, but I'm not sure exactly what. Anything would be better than sitting about uselessly. A lot of questions have been answered today, but not the most important one.

Where is Mum?

I don't know why, but when I go back upstairs, I log into the Scrabble site. Alex's ID icon is green. I almost knew for certain it would be.

Finlay?

I ignore her. If it even is her, and not her dad. I'm going to delete my account.

Are you OK?

Against my better judgement I send a snappy reply back: **What do you care?**

I'm sorry.

I want to be angry at her, to tell her to just get lost, but I can't help but remember the terror on her face when her dad appeared in the park.

I want to tell you some stuff about your mum. Stuff I didn't dare say in front of Dad.

I'm not going to fall for *that* again. **Don't bother**, I type. **I'm done.**

He threatened her, Finlay. Her reply comes back right away, before I can close the window. **She left to protect you both.**

My whole body feels wobbly and my hands are shaking so badly I can't type anything.

He told her he'd hurt you and your dad if she went to the police or showed her face ever again. It's the truth, Finlay. I'm so sorry.

I shut the message box and delete my account.

Monday, 25 May
Dear Mum,

After what happened in the park today, I thought I was OK, thought I'd taken it all in my stride. But later, when I went to bed, I found myself SOBBING [12] into my pillow.

I keep thinking about Alex, being stuck with that thug of a father. I'm so angry about what she did. But I don't think she's a bad person. I just don't think she had a choice.

Like you didn't think you had a choice. But you did. And you still do.

It's the Scrabble championships in two days. There's been so much going on I'd almost forgotten about it. I realize now it was just a silly dream, thinking I could win and that you'd see me, wherever you are and come back.

I've decided not to go.

I want to be around in case the police need to speak to me.

For the first time, I think I'm beginning to understand why you felt it was impossible for you to stay.

Your son,

Finlay

SCRABBLE WAS ORIGINALLY NAMED 'LEXICO'.

Tuesday

My alarm goes off. I hit 'snooze' and pull the covers over my head.

The first train whooshes by at 6.05 a.m. and I think about all those people already on their way somewhere, dressed and out of the house. Wondering what their day will bring.

At nine o'clock Dad taps on my door.

'Finlay? Mrs Adams just rang. You're supposed to be at the youth club now, playing practice matches for tomorrow's championships.'

'I'm n-not going,' I say, my words muffled by the pillow.

'Are you ill?'

'N-no. Y-yes, I'm f-feeling s-sick.' Which is true.

I hear my bedroom door open and Dad comes into the room.

'Let's have a look at you, then.'

I stick my head out of the covers.

'You look all right to me, lad.'

'I'm n-not,' I say.

Dad sits on the end of my bed. 'I know all this is unsettling . . . but it'll all come out in the wash, son.'

'It fl-flaming won't,' I cry, suddenly wanting to lash out and kick him off my bed. 'Y-you always s-say it will b-be all right and s-sometimes it j-just isn't.'

Dad's eyes widen at my outburst and then he looks down at his hands.

'You're right,' he says quietly. 'I think it's a case of me saying it because that's what I'm praying for.'

'P-praying might n-not be enough, D-Dad,' I say. 'M-Mum could be in r-real danger.'

Dad winces at the mention of Mum, and that makes me angrier. Even though the idea that Mum had an affair with King makes me feel sick, I still need to know she's OK.

'Th-this is your f-fault,' I shout, sitting up in bed. 'If y-you'd talked about it, m-maybe we c-could've found her b-before n-now.'

I expect him to start swearing, defending himself, before storming out. But he doesn't do any of those things. He looks at me, and I look back at him, and his face kind of looks all squashed up, like there's nothing solid holding it up underneath.

'I loved her, Finlay. I loved your mum more than

anything. For months after she left, I cried myself to sleep at night. I had to push the memory of what she'd done away. I had to do it to keep my sanity.' He reaches for my hand and squeezes my balled fist. 'I'm sorry, son. It was selfish of me but I had to find a way to keep going, you know?'

He presses a knuckle against his lips. 'I wanted to talk to you about everything that had happened, I planned to – I swear that's the truth. I didn't know anything about the fraud she'd uncovered at work. If I had, it might've shocked me into doing something. I might have realized that King was trying to blackmail her to keep quiet about something more than . . .' He trails off and scrubs at the carpet with his foot. 'If I'd fought to keep her here, she might have told me more, but I just thought . . . if she wanted to leave so much, how could I stop her? I'll never forgive myself for that.'

We sit for a while, with Dad just holding my hand. His grip is strong and sure, and I feel better for it. For what must be the first time since I can remember, he doesn't smell of cigarette smoke.

'Now get ready and I'll run you to the youth club,' he says finally, standing up.

'I-I'm not g-going,' I say.

'Fair enough, I'm not going to argue with you. But you're daft not getting some practice in for tomorrow.'

'I-I'm not g-going t-tomorrow,' I say.

Dad sits down again.

'Bloody hell, Finlay,' he says.

I shrug and pick at the stitching on my quilt cover. It's the Ninja Turtle one Mum bought me for my eleventh birthday. I'm way too old for it now, but since Mum went, some things have just stayed frozen in time.

'Your mother would be fuming,' Dad says. 'She'd raise the roof, turning an opportunity like this down.'

He's right, she would. But she isn't here.

'You've got a talent for it,' Dad says. 'Words. That's your skill.'

That's a laugh. Words torture me every day of my life. Besides, he's only ever wanted me to be good at football and he knows it. He's never even seen me play Scrabble.

'Look, I know I haven't been your best supporter,' Dad says awkwardly. 'But Mrs Adams . . . well, she says you're up there with the best in the country. That's one hell of a compliment, lad.'

'I w-want to be ar-around if the p-police need us,' I say.

'You heard what the coppers said, there's a lot of work, a lot of investigating to take place. One day isn't going to make any difference.'

I can't believe Dad is actually trying to convince me to play Scrabble when he's spent the last few weeks concerned that I should be out playing footy with my non-existent mates.

'Look, how's this?' he says, twisting to face me. 'I'll come with you, to support you, like. I'll have my phone with me so we won't miss anything the police might want to tell us.'

I've never known Dad take time off work to do something together. Yes, he's moped around for the last few days, but his diary is full again and he's been back working since talking to the police after the break-in.

'Y-you'll come to B-Birmingham?'

'Yep. And I'll stay all day. That's supposing you're not knocked out first round, mind.' He grins. 'I've done my best for you, son, but that best hasn't been nearly good enough. And . . . I'm sorry for that.'

I can't speak. Not for a few moments.

'D-deal,' I manage eventually, hardly able to believe he means it.

'Now, get dressed and let's get you to that youth club.' Dad grins, standing up again. 'And I'll nip out and do a bit of clothes shopping while you're there.'

Dad hasn't bought new clothes for *at least* two years.

'What's that look for?' Dad says, pretending to be affronted. 'We can't have the winner's dad looking less than smart, can we, lad?

Tuesday, 26 May

Dear Mum,

So it turns out I am going to the championships after all. I had a good practice session at the youth club with Maryam, so I'm as prepared as I'll ever be, I guess.

It's funny how much things have changed. Now the police are involved, for the first time I really feel like it won't be long until we find out where you have been for the last two years. I know we're going to find some answers, even though I'm scared they might not be the ones I'm hoping for.

Whatever happens, I've decided this will be my final journal entry to you.

I've written an envelope, I've stuck on the stamps, and Dad has given me your PO Box address. When I've finished writing today, I'm taking the journal to the post box at the end of our street.

It will all be down to you then, Mum.

If the police can't find you, if I don't win the championship and get into the papers, and if you reading this journal doesn't work, I suppose it's time to admit that nothing will.

It's hard to separate what's true and what are lies any more. I've realized that, sometimes, the only thing you can do is just accept that people do the best they can at the time. I'm talking about Dad mostly, but

I guess you did the best you could, too.

It's hard to imagine how bad things must have got in order for you to just walk out. And some of the stuff I've heard, I can't believe you'd do. Like having an affair with that PSYCHO [16], King. But there's one thing that shines through all the darkness like a beam of light. Remember what it is when you read this journal.

You're my mum. You'll always be my mum.

No matter how awful the truth turns out to be, I will always love you.

Love,

Finlay x

BEGINNER PLAYERS SHOULD LEARN THE TWO-LETTER WORDS TO MAXIMIZE THEIR PLAYING CHANCES.

Wednesday

The school minibus holds sixteen people and it's jam-packed full.

There's me, Maryam and Dad, Mrs Adams, and most of the after-school Scrabble club members too.

'They all want to come and support you,' Mrs Adams had said yesterday at training.

On the one hand, it's really nice that everyone wants to come along. On the other, it means more pressure.

'By the way,' Maryam says as we shuffle to get comfy in the small seats. 'I want you to know that I have got your back. I think that is the correct phrase.'

I frown at her, not understanding.

'I have agreed to act as the school's substitute player in the absence of Oliver.' She grins. 'I have always said my playing days were behind me, but for you, my friend, I shall make an exception this once. Although of course I know I will not be required to play because you will win every game, no problem.'

'Th-thanks.' I smile. I know Maryam wouldn't do this for anybody else and it feels good that we're a team today. There isn't anyone I'd rather have on my side.

The driver puts the radio on and everybody starts chattering. Dad and a teacher who's come along discuss Nottingham Forest's latest games and Maryam throws me some words for last-minute anagram training.

Just over an hour later, the minibus pulls up outside the Britannia Hotel in Birmingham. It's a big, tall old building with fancy shops on the ground floor.

A twitchy fluttering starts up in my belly, making me want to dash for the loo.

Mrs Adams tells us all to stay seated and pops into the hotel foyer to confirm arrangements. Two minutes later she's back, and the driver heads round to the car park at the rear. When the minibus turns into the parking area, we all sit up straight and gape. The area is a seething mass of people and parked coaches. Officials in green blazers are dotted around, taking names and consulting their clipboards.

All different kinds of people in all different kinds of uniforms gather in groups, chattering excitedly.

That's when I realize the scale of the event.

And that's when I start to feel a bit sick.

OK, a lot sick.

*

'You feeling all right, lad?' Dad asks me half an hour later when we're registered and queuing to gain entrance to the large function room of the hotel, where the first rounds of the championships will take place.

'F-fine, th-thanks,' I say, looking straight ahead.

My legs feel restless; they want to walk, to stride away from here but I hold them firm. It's just my nervousness making itself known.

'It's OK to be scared, you know,' Dad says, nudging me with his elbow. 'I remember my first football trial. I stayed up nearly all night, belting in goals non-stop on the local playing field, so I could make the High School team.'

I look at Dad with interest. He's never told me stuff like this before.

'And d-did you?' I say.

'Did I what?'

'M-make the t-trial?'

'Nah, I was that terrified on the day of the trial, I got the runs and your nan wouldn't let me go.' Dad always says 'your nan', like we were close, but she died before I was born.

Mrs Adams appears with a name badge, just as we reach the door to the competition hall. 'You should be very proud to represent Carlton Comprehensive, Finlay,' she says, as she pins it on to my blazer. 'He's going to do us proud. Right, Mr McIntosh?'

'Oh, aye. Our Finlay's no quitter, he'll eat this lot for breakfast.'

I follow Dad's eyes as he scans the enormous room. My stomach lurches like I've just climbed on to a speedboat. It looks just like the examinations hall at school. Tables set out in rigid lines and officials dressed in blazers stalking up and down the walkways in between them. The Scrabble players are starting to take their seats at the tables and it suddenly hits me why my nerves are shredded. They all look so much older than me.

'Are w-we in the r-right bit of th-the c-competition?' I whisper to Maryam, who has just appeared at my side. 'Th-that boy over there l-looks ab-about eighteen.'

'He probably *is* eighteen.' Maryam grins. 'Anyone up to the age of eighteen can play in the youth championships.'

I gulp. How will I have a chance if I'm drawn against someone *that* much older with all that game experience?

'Remember, you often beat me quite easily, Finlay,' Maryam whispers in my ear, as though she has read my mind.

It's true, I have. But when I play Maryam, I don't feel sick or shake like a jellyfish operating a road digger.

Maryam excuses herself to use the bathroom and Mrs Adams dashes off to confirm exactly where I'm sitting. I turn round to speak to Dad but he's wandered off back into the foyer, nattering on his phone. I'm aware of the people around me moving aside for something or somebody to come through and I do the same out of instinct.

Through the parting crowd, a tall older boy approaches. He wears an expensive-looking burgundy school blazer, complete with dark green and mustard striped lapels. He is flanked by a group of similarly dressed boys but even though I don't know him, there is something about him that draws my eye. He walks like he is entitled, like he fully expects others to stand back and let him pass. Which is, in actual fact, what we are all doing.

'That's Amos Best,' I hear a girl behind me stage-whisper to her friend. 'Last year's champion.' One of the boys in his entourage looks over at me and whispers something to Amos, causing him to chuckle.

When the group gets closer, Amos sweeps his hand over an already immaculate raven-haired quiff and smirks at me. He points towards the foyer. 'You'll find the crèche is that way, little boy,' he says in a clipped, nasal accent. The whole group laugh and push roughly past me. I watch as he takes his seat at a table in the far corner of the hall.

I look around to see if Mrs Adams is on her way back yet. My heart thumps madly when I catch sight of Maryam, hemmed close to the wall by a boy and a man. For a few seconds I freeze, hardly able to believe what I'm seeing, and then something in me springs into action and I push my way through the glut of people still queuing to get into the competition hall.

'Finlay!' I look back over my shoulder to see Mrs Adams waving at me. 'You need to take your place now,' she shouts.

I hold my hand up to signal I've heard her and carry on pushing forward, towards the foyer where Maryam stands, her eyes downcast.

'S' IS ONE OF THE MOST POPULAR STARTING LETTERS FOR WORDS.

It seems to take forever to push through the crowd. All my worries about the championships are forgotten in a hot flush of anger as I recognize the two people bothering her.

'L-leave h-her alone,' I snap when I finally get close.

My voice trails off when Oliver turns to look at me. His face is a mass of blue and yellow bruises. One eye is still nearly closed and a large patch of hair has been shaved from the side of his head. A row of tape covers what I assume to be stitches. Shock freezes my face. I never imagined his injuries to be so bad.

'Who's this?' Oliver's dad frowns, towering above me.

'Hello, Finlay,' Oliver says. 'We were just talking to Maryam.' His voice sounds thin and reedy, like someone sucked all the filling out of his words.

I open my mouth and look at Oliver and his dad. The silence sticks us together like glue, waiting to catch the blundering words I'm swallowing back.

'If you've got summat to say, then say it.' Oliver's dad peers at my face as if he's trying to pinpoint exactly where the problem lies.

'C-come on, M-Maryam,' I say, reaching for her arm. 'Let's g-go. You d-don't have to l-listen to –'

'Now, just a minute,' Oliver's dad says. 'Just hold your horses and listen to what our Oliver's got to say.'

'N-no! W-we've l-listened en-enough –'

'It's OK, Finlay,' Maryam says in a small voice. 'Oliver is apologizing.'

Apologizing? Oliver?

'Like I said . . . I'm sorry for the things I said to you in the library,' Oliver says in his strange, new voice. 'I didn't know that the reason you came over here was for your dad to work at the hospital. I mean, I thought people like you just –'

'People like me?' Maryam's eyes flash.

Oliver's dad coughs.

'What he means is, we realize now you're not like the others, like. You're different.'

'The others?' Maryam asks, her eyes wide.

I bite my bottom lip. Oliver and his dad are trying to make amends but they're just digging themselves into a deeper hole.

'You know, immigrants; them that come over here just for benefits,' Oliver's dad says cheerfully. 'You're not like them, is what we're saying. We welcome people like your dad in our country.'

'There are refugees here, if that's what you mean, Mr Haywood. People who've lost their homes and are fleeing for their lives,' Maryam says, looking from Oliver to his dad. 'It doesn't mean they have any less right to be here than myself and my family.'

No meek Maryam today. She's speaking out loud and clear, looking them both in the eye.

'Course not, course not,' Mr Haywood says hastily. 'We just wanted you to know we're very grateful for what your old man did for our Oliver and that we know you haven't just come over here after an easy life.'

Maryam shakes her head and rolls her eyes up to the ceiling as though there's no hope to be found.

'Maryam's dad saved Oliver's life,' he says, turning to me. 'If Ollie hadn't had that operation when he did, well . . .' Mr Haywood's voice wavers and he stops speaking.

It had slipped my mind that Maryam's father worked at the Queen's Medical Centre. Seeing Oliver so weak and broken sends a shiver down my spine.

'Maryam's dad is a specialist brain trauma surgeon,' Oliver tells me, looking over at her. 'Without him, I would've had to be transferred to another hospital, and it might've been too late for me.'

'I'm very pleased to see you are OK,' Maryam says graciously. 'And I accept your apology, Oliver. Maybe when you are better, we can have a proper conversation about *those people*.'

'Er, OK.' Oliver turns to me. 'Finlay, I've been – well, I mean, I admit –'

'W-why did y-you run in fr-front of the c-car?' I interrupt. I can hardly bear to look at this new, broken Oliver.

'I can't remember,' Oliver says. He shrugs and winces at the pain of the movement. 'I can't remember anything about it at all.'

'The doctors say his memory should come back,' Mr Haywood says. 'He remembered some bits just after the accident . . . but after he lost consciousness, it went.'

'Being in hospital gives you lots of thinking time,' Oliver continues. 'I asked Dad to bring me today because, well, I wanted to see you whip everyone's ass.' He grins at me.

I'm so surprised I don't even manage to say anything back.

Just then Mrs Adams rushes up, out of breath. 'Finlay, you need to come and take your place in the competition hall *now*, no excuses.' She follows my eyes as I glance at the others. 'Oliver! What are you doing here?' She stares in silent shock at Oliver's injuries and her face creases in concern. 'Is Oliver fit to be here, Mr Haywood?'

'Not really,' Oliver's dad admits. 'But he insisted on coming and the doctors agreed to let him out. Just for the afternoon, mind. He had something to say to Maryam and he wanted to support Finlay today, in his first few games.'

'Well, we're very pleased to see you, Oliver,' Mrs Adams says. 'Follow us into the hall and I'll make sure you get a spectator seat near Finlay's table.'

'You n-never said your d-dad op-operated on Oliver,' I say to Maryam, as we walk behind them to the hall.

'I didn't know,' Maryam says. 'My father never speaks about his work at home.'

As we enter the competition area again, Maryam has to nudge me gently to keep me moving forward. The hall is heaving. Most of the contestants are seated now and I follow Mrs Adams over to one of the middle rows.

I sit down in my seat and the dark-haired boy opposite offers his hand.

'Henry Dillingham,' he says. 'St Michael's Boys', in Kent.'

I take a big breath and pray the words will tumble out in the right order.

'Finlay-McIntosh-Carlton-Comp.' Despite managing to get all the words out in one breath, they tumble and knock into each other and don't sound quite right. Henry looks at me a second too long. He knows there's something different about me but he's not sure what.

I hate meeting new people. In a split second they all label me an idiot and a freak. That's what they'll all

270

think if I win and I have to speak in public.

I reach for the tile bag and we select letters.

'The rules are very strict in competitions,' Mrs Adams had explained when I asked if I could bring my own tile bag. 'Only authorized championship equipment is allowed, I'm afraid.'

An ancient-looking bloke at the front says a few words about the event and then everyone claps and he declares the championships open. Henry draws first turn. He starts the clock and we're off.

I see Maryam and Dad, Mrs Adams and Oliver out of the corner of my eye. They're all watching and willing me to win. I purposely don't smile or wave back. I put on my imaginary blinkers and focus on the game, cutting everything else off.

Henry plays G-U-L-L-E-Y [11]. I'm stunned to see he places the E, worth one point, on the double-letter tile, instead of the Y, which is worth four points.

I come back with F-U-G [13], tying up Henry's U and using a double-letter tile on the F and the G.

I see a tell-tale frown flit briefly over his face and that's when I know. He has no vowels on his letter rack. He's also very nervous – as I am. The difference is he's already letting it affect his play.

I decide to ramp up my play speed to increase the pressure on him and I'll also try to tie up all vowels at every available opportunity.

It's then that I realize something amazing.

Thanks to Maryam's training, I'm reading him like a book.

SCRABBLE CAN BE USED TO INCREASE ONE'S VOCABULARY.

I comfortably win the game with Henry and also the matches with Christian from St Ives, Nigel from Leeds and Katie from St Helen's.

Their ages range from fifteen to seventeen.

But I don't care about ages any more. All I care about is winning.

And after that, all I care about is finding Mum.

We break for lunch and Maryam rushes over. 'Finlay, you are doing amazingly. You are remembering all the training. I am so impressed!'

'Brilliant, Finlay.' Mrs Adams pats me on the back. 'You're doing yourself and the school proud. Keep it up.'

Oliver and his dad walk over. Oliver shuffles along slowly, like he is at the end of a long journey. 'You did fantastic.' He yawns behind his hand. 'Keep practising and you might be as good as me, one day.'

Everyone laughs, including Oliver, and strangely,

I find myself relieved to see some of the old him still remains.

'Come on, then,' his dad calls. 'Let's get you back, else the doctors will have my guts for garters.'

We all say our goodbyes and head for the reception to eat the sandwiches that Maryam's mum has made for us.

'H-how far is Wa-Walsall from h-here?' I ask Mrs Adams when Maryam and Dad are talking.

'Hmm, not sure Finlay, maybe six or seven miles. Why?'

'J-just w-wondered.' I shrug.

As I eat, I watch people milling around in reception. Women with their backs to me, Mum's build but with a different hair colour and style. Hair can easily be changed. What if one of them *was* Mum? What if she'd come to watch the championships and doesn't realize I'm here?

I stand up, ready to walk into the crowd. Mrs Adams jumps up, too. 'Right, just a few minutes to spare for a toilet break and then we'll head back in,' she says.

My third game after lunch is with a pale, thin girl called Lucy. She barely looks at me, she's so focused on the board. If I can win this game, I'm in the last handful of players. Even as I think it, I can hardly believe it.

Lucy is a very good player. She's better than the people I've played so far, but that's no surprise. The net is getting smaller all the time, soon there'll just be winners left, to battle it out against each other.

We're ten minutes in and at level pegging, 220–224 to me.

I watch Lucy's face and although, like a good player, she keeps her expression fairly blank, I see an unmistakable look of glee flicker suddenly in her eyes and I know something big is coming.

She uses the S from the word I just played, to make Z-E-B-E-C-K-S and she lands the B and the C both on a double-letter square.

'Thirty points,' I hear her whisper under her breath, like she's telling herself a delicious secret.

I glance at the game clock. There's only five minutes play left and it's my turn. Lucy sits back in her chair, yawns and stretches. She thinks the game is over. She's written me off. I know this is my last turn because when I play my word, Lucy will just stretch her turn out until the clock pings, ensuring I don't get another go. Whatever I play has got to be *amazing* for me to win . . . and there lies the problem.

I haven't got a word.

I haven't even got a low-scoring word that can run off one of Lucy's. My letters are all disjointed and refuse to latch on to each other. I stare at the board and wait for building opportunities to make themselves known to me, wait for my brain to do its job and pick up a familiar space or pattern that I can fill with a word.

But none of this happens.

Maryam's words echo in my head.

The most obvious action is not always the most effective.

'You played a good game.' Lucy's thin lips press together. 'Don't beat yourself up.'

I don't acknowledge her because I'm too busy thinking. An idea is trickling into my mind like water into parched earth. I wait and wait and suddenly, it all clicks into place like the pieces of a puzzle.

I pick up four letters and lay them down the side of Lucy's word ZEBECKS. My word is A-X-O-N.

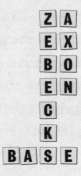

Lucy stops yawning and sits upright.

I can see by her face she's already calculated that I get twenty-seven points for AXON, landing my X on a triple-letter square. And I also get four two-letter words – ZA, EX, BO and EN – totalling forty-two points.

Grand total = sixty-nine points.

A smattering of applause comes from the people standing near our table.

The clock beeps, signalling the end of our game.

When I look up, Dad smiles and quickly wipes the corner of his eye when he lifts his hand up to scratch his head.

YOU DO NOT HAVE TO KNOW THE
MEANING OF A WORD TO PLAY IT.

After that last game, I'm grateful for the afternoon break. My head feels liked it's filled with porridge.

Mrs Adams is demented with the excitement of my win. 'Right, we need a strategy, Finlay,' she keeps repeating, while I crunch my way through a bag of crisps. 'We need a failsafe strategy. What's your approach for –'

'I d-don't know,' I say with my mouth full.

I'm surprised how much energy playing in the championship takes. I'm surprised I'm hungry because my insides feel like they're slowly turning to liquid.

'He changes his strategy according to his opponent,' Maryam explains, as if Mrs Adams is a novice.

'Good plan that, Finlay,' Dad nods. 'You do right with that approach, lad.'

Mrs Adams studies a clutch of papers in her hands for a few moments before looking at me again. 'Two more games, Finlay. Play two more games like that one and you've –'

'W-won?'

'No, you'll have made the final two, I was going to say.'

I nod. Sounds easy, the way Mrs Adams puts it.

But two more games and maybe . . . just maybe . . . I might get to see Mum again.

'Just getting to the final would make school history,' Mrs Adams comments. 'Nobody has ever —'

'D-done it b-before?' I interrupt.

'Yes, that's what I was about to say, if you'd just let me speak,' Mrs Adams snaps.

'I-irritating isn't it, wh-when people d-don't let you f-finish wh-what you w-wanted to s-say?' I grin at her.

Maryam winks at me over Mrs Adams's shoulder.

Mrs Adams's eyes widen and she gives me a short nod. 'Point taken, Finlay.'

I win the next game easily enough. My opponent is a seventeen-year-old boy from Aberdeen, called Christopher.

'I've got a bad cold,' he says when he gets up from the table after my win. 'Let's see how good *you* are next year if you have a bad week.'

I think about a couple of days ago, when Alex's dad was trying his best to throttle me in that den. Not exactly what I'd class as a good week.

The steward points me to the next table where a petite

girl with long black hair and almond-shaped eyes sits, stroking a doll's hair. I offer my hand but she doesn't look up; she's totally focused on the doll. It's quite unnerving.

Just before we start, she looks up and narrows her eyes. 'You can't beat us. You can't beat us,' she hisses, and places the doll on her knee so its glassy eyes seem to be watching me.

And then she carries on playing as normal, apart from asking the doll's advice on various turns. We're at fairly level pegging throughout and then I manage to pull forward at the end, playing J-E-L-L-Y on a double-word square, netting me a cool thirty points.

When we both stand up and shake hands, I can't resist patting the doll on its head.

She snatches it away from me and stalks off.

'She's freaked out most of her opponents today with that doll.' Mrs Adams frowns, watching her walk away. 'I shall be putting in a formal complaint about her tactics.'

Maryam grins. 'Congratulations, Finlay. The final is yours for the taking. Two great wordsmiths, with the only difference being in *here*.' She taps her head. 'This is where you will win.'

'Proud of you, lad.' Dad grabs me in an awkward bear hug. His voice cracks but we both pretend not to notice.

The steward walks over, pen poised over his clipboard. 'Finlay McIntosh from Carlton Comprehensive, Nottingham?'

I nod.

'Congratulations, you made the final. Follow me, please.' I follow him up to the top of the hall, where a game table has been set up, apart from the others. 'Take your seat. The other player is just in the bathroom.'

The board, with its familiar colours and a layout I could sketch from memory, lies flat and blank before me. I wish I had my tile bag, just so I could feel Mum is with me and in some way, spurring me on.

I look up to see where Dad, Maryam and Mrs Adams are sitting and dozens of pairs of eyes meet mine. People are crowding around to watch. My breathing is getting heavier, like I'm doing physical exercise. But of course I'm just sitting, waiting for the biggest chance I ever had in my life to happen.

I spot movement at the hall doors, a small group of people pushing through and walking over to the finals table. And then I see him, head and shoulders above his friends and gliding towards me like a young king.

'Your opponent,' the steward announces. 'Amos Best.'

'The current champion,' Amos whispers as he shakes my hand and smiles for someone taking a photograph. 'But I'm in a good mood, so I'll try not to humiliate you *too* badly.'

The ancient-looking man stands up shakily and walks to the front of our table. 'I'm very proud to announce the start of this year's final, between –' he peers at a piece of paper in his quivering hand – 'Amos Best on the left of the table, aged eighteen, from Kent, and our current reigning champion. And on the right, Finlay McIntosh, aged fourteen, from Nottingham.'

The crowd applaud us and Amos takes his chance to lean forward. 'Tell me, little boy, has your voice broken yet, or does your stammer prevent it?' I hold out my hand to shake his and he grasps it so hard, my eyes sting. 'You can't even speak, so I doubt you can win,' he says between bared teeth that looks like a smile to everyone else.

I look at his greased-back hair, his immaculate clothes, his handsome face and I think: *I can win. Because you don't know what I know.* He doesn't know about struggle and pain and loss. He doesn't know how it feels to get through a day that feels like it's a month long.

To Amos Best, this is just a game.

To me, it is my whole life.

ANAGRAM TRAINING CAN REALLY IMPROVE A PLAYER'S GAME.

Amos draws first turn. I can tell from the gleeful look on his face that the letters he's picked must be truly spectacular. He barely hesitates, laying out the entire seven letters of his rack across the middle of the board. As he lays down his last letter and moves his hand, the word hits me like an uppercut to the chin.

S-T-A-M-M-E-R

I hear Maryam gasp and when I look over, Dad's face is dark and grim.

'Bingo!' he hisses.

Placing an M on a double-letter square and using all seven letters with its fifty-point bonus wins Amos a score of seventy-eight points.

I close my eyes for a second, removing Dad's face and Maryam's shock. *Focus, focus, focus* is all that counts. I can only win by playing as if nothing else exists.

'Your turn,' Amos says, plunging his hand into the tile bag.

I tag an S on the end of Amos's word and place S-T-U-C-K vertically down the edge of the board. It scores sixteen but I've included a triple-word square, so that multiplies my score up to forty-eight.

It's a left hook to his head. I catch Amos's smirk waver just a touch, before he comes back with P-U-C-K, using my K and pulling in a double-word square to score a very respectable twenty-four points.

And so it goes. The game is moving swiftly and I soon realize that Amos is forming better, more complicated words than I am. For the next few turns, each word he plays brings over twelve points, landing big blows to my head in our virtual boxing match.

But I know from watching boxing with Dad when I was younger that it is rarely the best strategy to chase the knockout punch. Most matches are won by constant well-placed blows to the body. They might not look as fancy or as dramatic, but their effects can be devastating.

'Running out of ideas?' Amos grins as he waits for me to play. 'I've already cleared a space on my trophy shelf at home. Don't prolong your agony, old chap.'

I select a letter and push it to the end of my rack with the other two that are already sitting there, purposely unused.

Then I play V-A-P-E, which earns me a respectable thirteen points using a double-letter square, but more importantly moves the game towards the left-hand side of the board.

Now Amos's words are looking less spectacular. He plays G-A-T-E, T-O-R-N and C-A-S-T up at the top of the board. I keep my play focused down at the bottom of the board, easing the tentacles of words over to the left-hand side.

With five minutes to go, the score is 260–473 to Amos.

He seems to be running out of options now but, confident with his comfortable lead, he continues to smirk throughout my play. I just pray he doesn't meddle with my set-up at the bottom of the board and nearly sigh with relief when he plays his next word at the top right of the board.

I'm aware of murmurs in the crowd, sure that the winner is clear.

Amos stops his clock and finally, the moment comes. It's my turn and I'm ready.

Everything is in place.

As I watch the red digits of the clock clicking through the seconds, I think about Maryam's Scrabble-board life-lesson. About the opportunities that lie among the everyday squares. A way to transform the ordinary into something special and, sometimes, into something that is truly amazing.

'Giving up, are we?' Amos says, leaning forward. 'I almost feel sorry that I've exposed your lack of skill so easily to the crowd.'

I hear him but the words don't mean anything. Nothing means anything but the picture I have in my head of Mum's face, reading the newspaper and seeing me. Running out of the house to find me.

My thoughts are interrupted by Amos sniggering. I follow his eyes to the clock which is telling me there is one minute left to play. I snap back to the game and select the letters I have been saving for this, my knockout punch to end the game.

Q-U-E-E-R-E-S-T

There is a collective gasp from the crowd and Amos's face turns long and pale.

Using the E of one of Amos's words, I stretch the word out from the bottom-left red triple-word square on the board to the middle triple-word square on the bottom row.

I look Amos directly in the eye.

'T-two hu-hundred and t-twelve p-points,' I say, jabbing my finger at Amos's first word in the centre of the board. 'Not a b-bad end to say w-we st-started with a st-stammer.'

THE IDEAL LETTER RACK CONSISTS OF SLIGHTLY MORE CONSONANTS THAN VOWELS.

I lose the game by one point to Amos. Dad is crying. I mean, properly crying. The tears are rolling down his face and he doesn't care who sees them. I look at him and I see his love for me, even though I lost.

'I'm so proud of you, son.' He pulls me into a hug.

'Th-thanks for c-coming, Dad,' I say.

Mrs Adams is scurrying around, trying to organize photographs of me with the other school Scrabble club members who came along to watch. When my dad finally lets me go she gives me an awkward squeeze. 'You were brilliant, Finlay,' she says.

'Th-thanks for b-b—' I take a deep breath,
Mrs Adams waits.

'Th-thanks for b-believing in m-me,' I say, finally.

'*You* did it all, Finlay,' she says. 'It's your achievement.'

'I l-lost.'

'By one point,' Maryam says from behind me. 'Your first time in a national championship and you lost by one point to the existing champion. I would certainly call that an achievement, Finlay.'

But the whole point of entering, so Mum would see me in the papers, see how brilliant I was and be desperate to come back, is over. I'm surrounded by piles of dead ends and false leads.

I look up as a microphone crackles into life. 'Please welcome Birmingham's Lord Mayor, who will now make the winner's presentation.'

The crowd erupts into applause and someone pushes me forward, back to the front of the hall. Amos stands next to the Lord Mayor, waving to the crowd, his face beaming.

'This way, Finlay,' someone calls and I see a photographer snapping away. On his camera is a sticker saying *The Birmingham Star*.

My heart swells. I wonder if there's still a chance Mum might see me after all.

After the photographs, Dad's strong arm grips mine and guides me away from the crowd.

Despite his new clothes and sprucing himself up, I can still smell the faint tang of creosote on his skin. People are calling me back.

'He needs a minute,' Dad replies, keeping me moving. 'Give him five.'

Dad leads me out of the hall and into a small side

room. My ears are ringing with the empty quiet of it. 'I've got something to tell you, lad,' he says, motioning for me to sit down. 'The police have arrested Alex's dad, Trevor King.' Dad shakes his head and sighs. 'It's over, son. He won't cause us any more hassle now.'

But it's not over really. Not until we find Mum. I feel like an old balloon, after all the air has leaked out. 'C-can we g-go home n-now?' I ask, trying to process what Dad's just told me.

'Soon, lad, soon. There's someone that you need to speak to first. Somebody I spoke to earlier.'

I remember how Dad stepped away from the hall this morning, deep in conversation on his phone. I groan and slump down further in my chair. I feel like this ordeal is never going to end.

Silence shrouds the room. Neither of us speaks.

Finally, I look up.

Dad is holding out his phone to me. I take it from him and hold it to my ear.

'Hello, Finlay,' a voice whispers.

SOMEWHERE IN THE WORLD THERE ARE OVER A MILLION MISSING SCRABBLE TILES.

All those times I've dreamed about finding Mum, hugging her and talking to her, now the moment has arrived, I just stand up and gape, too frightened to utter a word in case she disappears again.

'You were right, Finlay,' Dad says. 'Your mum has been living in Walsall.'

He gently removes the phone from my shaking hand and puts it on to loudspeaker.

Nothing fits together in my head, nothing makes sense at all. I feel like I'm watching everything from a distance, like I'm completely separate from myself.

I've got so much to say. I can't remember any of it.

'Finlay?' Mum whispers again, this time more urgent.

I don't think I can do it. I just don't know if I can. I take a big breath but nothing happens. The words I need to say are stuck to my tongue, my throat and the inside of my cheeks. They're clinging to me, desperate to stay inside.

But I have something to say. Something that's really important.

I take a deep breath.

'I-I've m-m-m—'

Another breath.

'I-I've m-missed you, M-Mum.'

I hear Mum sob.

I feel such a fool, sounding like a damaged soundtrack, but it's a soundtrack that I'm going to play, however long it takes.

'H-h-h—'

'Take your time, son,' Dad says, squeezing my arm.

Big breath.

'H-how-did-you-know —'

But I can't push any more words out.

'I picked up your dad's letter yesterday.' Mum's voice cracks. 'The police had already been in touch with the Post Office. The staff kept me there until they arrived. I'm so glad they did. If they'd tried to explain . . .' she trails off, holding back a sob.

I take a big breath and force out the words. 'Why-did-you-leave-without-saying-g-goodbye?'

There is silence on the end of the line. Dad closes his eyes.

I hear Mum take a deep breath. 'I would like to explain to you face to face, not now, not like this . . .'

'M-Mum,' I say firmly. 'I n-need to kn-know. N-now.'

There is a long pause. When she starts talking, her voice sounds small and scared. 'Sometimes, when you feel like the whole world is against you, it's easier to crawl away into the shadows than face up to what you've done,' Mum says, her voice shaking. 'I was so . . . *ashamed*.' The last word is a whisper.

Dad grabs my hand and grips it tight.

'I made a stupid, stupid mistake,' Mum whispers. 'I got myself involved with Trevor . . . Trevor King. Me and your dad, we – well, we were having some problems. But I did wrong, Finlay. It was my fault.'

I look at Dad. He still has his eyes closed.

'Y-you h-had an aff-affair?'

'I'm so sorry to say it . . . but I did. When I found out he was nothing but a cheating crook, I was going to turn him in to the police, but he threatened to tell you and your dad about what had happened between us . . .'

I'm desperately trying to fit the pieces together in my head about why she left, but it's still not working. I know she told Dad about the affair anyway.

'There's something else,' Mum says. I can almost feel the willpower she's using to force herself to get these words out. 'Something I just couldn't find the words to tell you both, back then.' She takes a shaky breath. 'I was pregnant. I knew if King found out he would never leave me alone, never leave us alone.'

'W-was it K-K-King's b-baby?' I choke.

Her silence is her answer.

I don't know what to say. I can't speak. Even though I can still hear the buzz of people talking in the big hall, it feels so lonely here, just me and Dad and a phone.

'I was so scared for you . . . your dad and the baby. I thought I was saving us all. I thought it would just be for a few weeks or so. I thought I would find the courage to come back. I realize now I was just running away. I was a coward.'

'You could've told me, Christa,' Dad's words sound strangled. 'I would have protected us all, you know that.'

There's a beat of silence and then Mum answers. 'King was a monster. I was terrified . . . And I believed him when he said he had a local copper on his payroll.' Her voice sounds frail and small. 'I even drove to the police station, do you know that? I walked in and said I wanted to make a statement. This policeman behind the counter, he looked at me funny. He walked into the back of the office and picked up the phone, staring at me the whole time. I couldn't risk it. If he'd have hurt either of you . . .'

I feel numb. But there are still things I need to know.

'Y-you hid the m-memory card so w-well, M-Mum – d-did you w-want us to f-find it?'

She says nothing, listening to me struggle with my words as if the struggle is hers. I can almost hear her biting back the tears.

'I hoped you'd never find it,' Mum says eventually.

'It was an insurance policy, in case King ever came after you or your dad. The copy of the original database was something I had over him . . . just in case . . . but he was never supposed to find out I had it. So I hid it where he would never look. You were never meant to find it.' Mum is quiet for a moment. 'I wanted to get back in touch, I need you both to know that. I never thought . . .' She starts crying, softly. 'The baby . . . he's eighteen months old now. His name is Miller.'

Dad and I stand side by side. Neither of us speaks, we just look at each other, taking her words all in, like we might only have these few precious minutes with her.

'Christa,' Dad says softly. 'We need to talk.'

'I'm on my way, the second I put down the phone,' she says. 'We'll see you both tonight . . . if that's OK with you?'

'Just hang tight for now,' Dad says softly. 'I'll call you later, OK?'

'OK,' whispers Mum, swallowing a sob. 'I'll be waiting.'

'M-Mum?' I cry out before Dad ends the call. 'I j-just w-wanted to s-say I'm s-sorry I d-didn't win the ch-champ-ion-sh-ships. I w-wanted to m-make you pr-proud of me. Every-th-thing w-was g-going to pl-plan and th-then —'

'Finlay,' Mum whispers, her voice cracking. 'There is nothing you could do to make me more proud of you than I already am. I love you with all my heart, whether you come first or last.'

Dad coughs and wipes at his eyes. 'Come on, son,' he mutters. 'Let's tell Mrs Adams we want to head home.'

'B-bye M-Mum,' I manage to whisper before he ends the call.

Back outside in the madness of the main hall, Dad and I get cornered by a BBC film crew as we make our way back to Mrs Adams.

'So, Finlay . . .' The presenter pushes a microphone in my face. 'What are your plans now, after missing out on being national champion by just one point?'

Faces surround us, hanging on to my every word.

I take a breath and I relax my shoulders. I ignore the itching in my arms.

'I'm g-going h-ho—' I don't apologize. I just keep trying. 'I'm g-going h-home.'

'What's it like, living with such a bad stammer, Finlay?' the presenter says, pushing the microphone closer. 'Has it affected your game?'

'Has it heck,' Dad snaps back. 'He only lost by one point. That's a winner in my book.'

'Has it put you off entering the competition again?' the reporter asks me, ignoring Dad.

'N-no,' I say, smiling back at the faces who seem to be willing me to say what I need to say. 'I'm ha-happy w-with sec-second pl-place be-because I g-gave it m-my all and th-that's all I c-can d-do.'

The reporter nods and smiles and the crowd applauds my answer. 'Well done, Finlay, you've done your school proud,' he says.

But I'm not listening. All I can think about is the fact that Mum has been found. At some point soon, maybe even tonight, I'm going to see her again . . . and meet my little half-brother. *My brother!* For the very first time.

Out of nowhere, Alex's face pops into my mind. I think about all the good chats we had, and her bruises and what her sad, pale face might look like if she knew about Miller, who is her half-brother, too.

'One last question, Finlay.' The reporter has my attention now. 'Can we expect to see you back again next year?' He pushes the microphone closer and the crowd falls quiet, waiting for my answer.

'J-just try and st-stop me.'

ACKNOWLEDGEMENTS

Thank you to beta readers Carol Roberts, Kalsuma Bibi and Shaju Hekim for their feedback, and also to Nick de Somogyi, the eagle-eyed copy-editor, who has worked on both *Smart* and *A Seven-Letter Word*.

I would like to extend heartfelt thanks to all the wonderful librarians who support and recommend my books, and to the young people in the many schools and academies I have visited and to those who have voted for *Smart* in so many awards . . . I look forward to meeting many more of you in the coming year.

Last but not least, thanks go to ALL my extended family, for supporting and believing in me, especially my lovely mum and my wonderful daughter, Francesca, for their regular pep talks, and to my husband, Mac, who is my rock and, among a thousand other things he does to make my life easier, supplies me with constant cups of tea while I shut myself away each day to write!

If you would like more information about or help with any of the issues covered in the book there are many excellent resources that can be accessed by searching online or, alternatively, ask a librarian, parent or teacher for help.

Finally, thank YOU for reading *A Seven-Letter Word*! If you enjoyed the book please contact me via Twitter, my website or my Facebook page to keep up to speed with my latest writing news!

www.kimslater.com

Read on for an exclusive extract
from *928 Miles from Home*

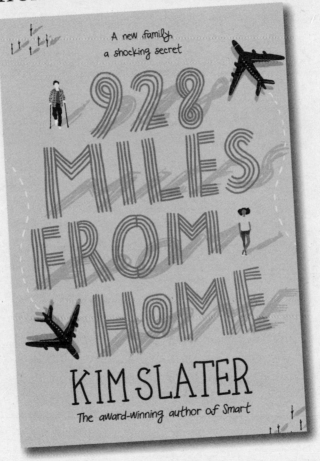

A new family
a shocking secret

928 MILES FROM HOME

KIM SLATER

The award-winning author of Smart

Journal Entry – July

Name: Calum Brooks
Age: 14

The school counsellor, Freya, has given me a brand-new notebook. It's one of those posh ones wrapped in cellophane.

Freya says I have to write in it every day, and that the most important thing to remember is to be completely honest, but the sort of thing I start thinking about is just stuff that nobody else would be interested in.

'Write whatever comes into your head and don't censor your feelings. If you want to write swear words or get mad and scrawl out a whole page, then that's OK,' Freya says in her soft Irish accent. 'It's your journal, Calum, so anything goes.'

Apparently, if she tells anybody else what we talk about, she'll be breaking some kind of counselling code and it could get her fired. 'I want you to know it's completely confidential,' she assures me again.

If the teachers were more laid-back like Freya, I might try a bit harder in class.

But I don't mind writing; in fact I really like it. And there's not much else to do now I'm stuck in this crummy flat with a broken leg.

Sometimes I make up scripts in my head, like I'm

writing a proper scene from a film. See, that's what I'd like to be: *a screenwriter*.

I know, I know. Despite what Sergei and Amelia say, it's a pretty stupid idea.

You don't see those sorts of vacancies down the jobcentre.

But I can't move and I'm bored out of my skull since the accident . . . so what have I got to lose?

Two Weeks Earlier

Mr Fox's room feels cold, and his booming voice echoes around the pale green, glossed walls so even though we're standing in a line, he seems to be all around us, all at once.

'You should all be ashamed of yourselves,' he says for the third time.

From where I'm standing at the end of the line, I can see the playing fields out of the small, paned window. The grass looks marshy and needs a cut. Some of the white markings on the pitch have worn away, leaving broken lines and fractured arcs that don't really mean anything any more.

Mr Fox is talking about integration and embracing change, and how this is 'the fabric our school has been built upon all these years'. Blah, blah, blah.

The wall in front of us is covered in dated black-and-white prints. Dusty frames containing old photographs of staff who must surely now be dead, and groups of smart young students who will now be old and grey.

I wonder briefly if in another fifty years, there will be boys who aren't even born yet, stood here in this very room getting a lecture like we are.

Mr Fox thumps the edge of his desk with his hand and glares at each of us in turn.

When he looks at me, I blink and scuff the toe of my shoe on the dark wiry carpet beneath my feet.

I can't say anything to Mr Fox in front of the others, but it's just not fair if *I* get excluded.

I just stood at the back of the group like I always do.

I didn't do any of the actual bullying.

We are stuck in Mr Fox's office for another twenty minutes trying to convince him of our innocence, but in the end, he issues all four of us with fixed-term exclusions.

I get kicked out for a day, Harry and Jack get two days each, and this time Linford is out for three days.

'I could have been harder on you all, but I've decided to be lenient on this occasion . . . on the proviso you sign up to see the school counsellor.' Mr Fox scowls. 'A warning. Next time you're in front of me – and there had better not be a next time – I'll be looking at permanent exclusions.'

He looks at Linford.

To be honest, I think Mr Fox is being really hard on us. I mean, the new lad was up on his feet in no time and once he stopped feeling dizzy, he just walked back to class. OK, he had a few bumps and bruises but nothing serious, not like when Linford kicked Karl Bingham so hard in the leg he fell off the climbing wall and broke his ankle.

Dad is working down south until Thursday, so when Mr Fox's exclusion letter drops through the letterbox, I'll just rip it up. Dad will be blissfully unaware that I've been in trouble at school.

I suppose that's *one* advantage to him working away most of the week.

In all the good films, people live in exciting places – the posh areas of London or America. Places I've never been and probably never will go because we live *here*.

Our flat in Nottingham is in St Ann's; an area that's been classed as 'deprived' by the government. What they really mean is that it's a dump, a slum-hole and best avoided by your average, decent person. People sort of get stuck here and your dreams get stuck too. *Dreams of the Deprived*: sounds like a pretty miserable movie title, doesn't it?

The people who actually live here don't call it deprived. We call it home.

It might not look it, with its boarded-up pubs and dated housing, but St Ann's is an OK place to be and most of our neighbours are decent. Folks might not drive fancy cars and wear top designer gear round here, but they're 'salt of the earth', as Grandad used to say.

We've got our problems like everywhere else, but

those of us who've lived around here for a long time, well I suppose we sort of look out for each other.

Like last year, when Dad was working down south for ten days.

★

EXT. ST ANN'S - DAY
Council Estate, December. Freezing cold, snowing, no cars on road. Everything covered in a blanket of fresh snow. Silent.

Starving BOY walks down road in knee-deep snow and hammers on door of first-floor flat.

MRS BREWSTER
(*from inside flat*)
Who the flippin' hell is it?

BOY
It's me, Calum, from number five.

MRS BREWSTER opens door. Hair in rollers, floral headscarf, ash on her cigarette a centimetre long. Pokes head out and squints at the bright whiteness.

MRS BREWSTER

What ya standing there wi' ya gob wide open
for?

BOY

Errm . . . the Happy Shopper has run out of
milk and bread.

(Starving BOY neglects to mention Dad is
away and money has run out.)

MRS BREWSTER
(*with a sympathetic smile*)
Just a sec.

Moments later, she reappears at door.

MRS BREWSTER
Here, tek these, mi duck.

She presses milk and half a loaf into
starving BOY's hands.

MRS BREWSTER
Come back if you need owt else.

END SCENE.

★

You get the picture.

Living here, you're not likely to get invited round for a cup of Earl Grey and a cucumber sandwich too often, but people still care about each other.

My mum took off with another bloke eleven years ago when I was still at nursery school. I can't remember her at all, although I know Dad's got a few photos put away somewhere.

I think that might be something I could put in my journal that Freya would find interesting. Counsellors like that sort of thing.

I've not told anybody this, but I dream about Mum now and then. She's just a presence rather than a person. A clean scent like soap or wash powder, a softness on my cheek.

Sometimes I wake up crying, but I never remember her face.

There's no way I'm writing any of that down; it sounds like one of those reality-TV sob stories. I don't want Freya thinking I'm soft.

So, maybe I could write about Dad.

My dad leaves a lot to be desired when it comes to parenting, but he's raised me – well, more like dragged me up – all on his own since Mum left.

We stick together, me and my dad. So far, we've managed to get by.

About the author

Kim Slater honed her storytelling skills as a child, writing macabre tales specially designed to scare her younger brother! Taking her literary inspiration from everyday life, Kim's debut novel, *Smart*, won more than ten regional prizes and has been shortlisted for over twenty regional and national awards, including the Waterstones Children's Book Prize and the Federation of Children's Book Groups Prize. *Smart* was also longlisted for the 2015 CILIP Carnegie Medal. She has written four novels for Macmillan Children's Books set in her home town of Nottingham, where she lives with her husband.

www.kimslater.com

Also by Kim Slater

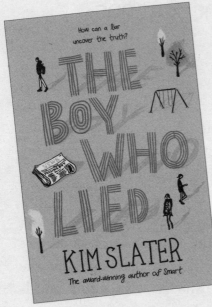